STAYING THE DISTANCE

A Novel by Franci McMahon

Firebrand
Books
Ithaca, New York

Book and cover design by Debra Engstrom
Cover photo by Ingelise Holst
Typesetting by Bets Ltd.

Library of Congress Cataloging-in-Publication Data

McMahon, Franci, 1941–
    Staying the distance : a novel / by Franci McMahon
      p.   cm.
    ISBN 1-56341-047-8 (cloth) — ISBN 1-56341-046-X (paper)
    1, Women ranchers—Montana—Fiction.   2. Ranch life—Montana-
-Fiction.   3. Lesbians—Montana—Fiction.   I. Title.
PS3563.C38557S7   1994
813'.54—dc20
                                                    93–49793
                                                         CIP

Acknowledgments

First, Barbara DuBois. Her editing skills and loving criticism kept pushing me further.

The following women gave me their responses to the manuscript: Joan Hamilton, who read six chapters aloud to me one evening; Ann Stokes, who helped me melt my stiffness in writing about sex; Hedy Harris, who tirelessly reread many chapters; Fran S., horse enthusiast, and Linda C., Montana native. There were also the dyke skiers in the ratty motel on our Yellowstone trip who listened to me read chapters out loud for the first time with wonderful reaction.

Carolyn Oliver never read a word of this book while it was in progress; however, she gave me enormous support and encouragement. Faye Des Moines helped me take myself seriously as a writer. Her early help was instrumental. The sensitive and professional editing skills of Nancy Bereano formed the manuscript into a book.

For guidance unleashing the mysteries of the Macintosh computer, and the use of their own, thanks to Jenny Eddy, Matthew, and Ian. And in Montana, Kerry Mulholand.

Kerry, again, and Suzanne Rice for all their superb support.

Jenifer Wise, who accented the Montana scenery for the book cover. And Ingelise Holst for photographing it.

Lisa, for telling me her dream.

The mysterious woman who anonymously gave me a grant. And Kestrel.

for Martha Aryes

One

The grey mare snorted her nostrils free of dust. Rachel Duncan let her stand and blow at the top of the ridge while she looked over the ranch for signs of the veterinarian's arrival. Even from this distance she could clearly see the ranch buildings—the house of log and stone cupped in the hand of thick fir and pine, its massive chimney on the north, its slanted roof lengthening out to form a front porch facing east; and the barn, not too far to walk to in thirty-five-below-zero winters, its lacework of pole corrals extending off to the south and west.

Only a few horses were visible in the corrals. Kate must have the others still shut in the barn, Rachel thought. On such a wonderful crisp spring day. Growling to herself about late, forgetful— yes, even senile—vets, she nudged Kestrel over the ridge and down the mile of slide and switchback to the ranch. At the barn, Rachel stepped off her horse with the casual ease of a horsewoman intimate with her companion. Neither looked as if they had just traveled some twenty-five miles over rough Montana landscape. Both in their prime—Rachel at forty-one, Kestrel at ten—they were in training for the toughest horse race of all, the Tevis Cup: one hundred miles in one day from Lake Tahoe over the Sierra Nevada Mountains to Auburn, California.

Kate met up with her at the hitching rail. "I'll turn Kestrel out into the field for you," she offered.

"No, thanks." Rachel's long, lean fingers slipped the latigo through the cinch ring and pulled the saddle off, catching the saddle blanket before it hit the ground. Her strong face was closed, the small lines around her eyes a little sharp.

Kate followed Rachel into the tack room to ask, as Rachel threw her saddle roughly onto the rack, "Hey, how was your ride? Kestrel going O.K.? She looks great to me."

Rachel stopped, settled her saddle into place, then looked at her ranch hand. "The mare is fine. Guess I'm a little annoyed Dr. Stewart isn't here yet. He call?" At Kate's negative shake, Rachel continued, "I'm hungry, too." She smiled slowly. "Feels like there's a wolf pack in there after my liver."

"There's some stew in the oven. It's all just routine stuff for the vet, isn't it? I can turn them loose if he doesn't show soon."

Rachel nodded, then leaned against the doorjamb and looked with sympathy at the corraled horses waiting for their spring shots and other medical care. She could faintly catch the grassy scent coming with the wind across the pastures. She went back out to her horse to sponge the sweat off with cool water, check her legs, then turn her out. At the gate, watching Kestrel canter off to join her herd, Rachel unzipped the long zippers running the length of her brown leather chaps on the outside of each leg. Slowly she unfastened the belt which rested just above her pubic bone, slung the chaps over her shoulder, and turned on the high heels of her Western boots.

She took the porch steps two at a time, then hung her chaps by the door on a peg burnished with use to a rich gloss. Years before, her grandfather had put a sink on the porch for the ranch hands to wash off the dust before coming into the kitchen for meals. It had eased some strife in the household at the time, and Rachel enjoyed using it, the single faucet's perpetually cold water marking summer's beginning and end.

Rachel rinsed off some of the dust and peered into the mirror, bobbing slightly between the areas that had lost their silver. She laughed at the shiny oval of eyes, nose, and mouth surrounded by fine white Montana face powder. I could try a little harder to look presentable to Dr. Stewart if he ever does come, she thought, dunking deeper into the water. Reaching for a towel, she glimpsed herself once again in the glass. This time she was unprepared, and stared, almost having forgotten what she looked like.

Sometimes Rachel liked the way she looked. Most times she

never thought about it. Standing about five-foot-nine, she was fairly lanky for her large frame. In an angular face, almost-connecting bushy eyebrows stood guard over brown-green brindle eyes, which narrowed to slits with radiating wrinkles when she was amused. Her wide mouth could look lean and stern or take up half her face when she laughed. At the moment, her waist-length hair, brown with a few streaks of grey, was making a concerted effort to escape from the braided knot that held it. Pushing some of the renegade hairs back behind her ears, she headed for the kitchen and Kate's promised stew.

A short time later, the stew settling into her, sitting back with her boots up on a chair, Rachel considered how lucky she was to have Kate at the ranch. Of all the horse-crazy teenage girls who had hung around and eventually come to work for her, Kate was the best, a true horsewoman. Her small frame, her height of five feet four inches, were perfect for starting young horses, which she did very well. At twenty-one, Kate knew college was not in her future. Of course she could attend the tribal college in Harlem, up on the high line, that northernmost strip of highway and towns before the Canadian border. But she didn't want to learn some job that would keep her sitting in a little chair with rollers. Once a month, Kate traveled to Rocky Boys Reservation where her grandmother lived to learn from her. Right now she was getting paid for what she liked doing most in the world.

And in the meantime, Rachel needed to solve the mystery of the missing vet. Let's list the possibilities, she thought. One, he's called out to an emergency in the opposite direction. Two, he drove off the road. Three, he forgot. Four, he ran into someone he knows and they're still standing there, talking about the most interesting prolapse they've ever seen. Glowering at her boot toes, she decided that while this all might be very interesting, it was getting her nowhere fast. For damn sure, she thought, if I turn those bangtails out on that fresh grass, his jeep will come dancing up the road just as the last tails go over the hill.

The whine of the jeep cut through Rachel's thoughts. She dropped her feet to the floor and stood in one fluid movement. By the time the screen door had banged shut behind her, the jeep was in the barnyard. She long-strided her way to the driver's side, intending to greet Dr. Stewart, but was brought to a full stop when she saw the lovely woman who was somewhat tiredly leaving the passenger side.

The woman laughed and asked, with an unmistakable Boston accent, "Aren't there any paved roads in this territory?" Under raised eyebrows, clear blue eyes looked at Rachel over the jeep's roof.

Before Rachel could think much beyond wondering what this exotic creature was doing in Montana, Dr. Stewart approached and said, "Rachel, I'd like you to meet Dr. Carson. I've been taking her on rounds so she can meet everyone before I leave."

"Well, it's great to hear you're finally taking a vacation. When do you start? And how long will you be gone?" Rachel felt a pang of anxiety.

There was a stunned look on Fred Stewart's face. "You mean I didn't tell you? How could I have not—" He flushed a deep red. "I'm sorry, Rachel, but I'm retiring to Arizona next week. This practice has gotten too hard—long hours, distances—and Dr. Carson here is eager to take it on. I sold the practice to her."

Rachel blurted out, "What about the Tevis Cup? What if Kestrel gets sick or. . ." Her voice tapered off.

"I don't think you need to worry. Dr. Carson will take good care of your horses. She graduated from Cornell with honors and with an equine specialty."

Rachel's good manners were engaged in a battle with the doubt and disappointment overwhelming her. She looked at the female veterinarian as she mouthed a greeting, thinking the woman would surely have to prove herself in this part of the country. Eyeing her surreptitiously on the way to the barn, Rachel saw the finely drawn features warmed by a tender mouth and framed by hair the most extraordinary color of yellow and red-gold. The way it was fashioned seemed very peculiar: a crew-cut in front—or the shortest bangs Rachel had ever seen—with a braid down the back almost to her waist. Suddenly Dr. Carson turned her head and the blue eyes were boring into Rachel, freezing her like a mongoose's prey.

Dr. Carson opened the barn door, and Rachel's feet slammed back to earth. She found herself casting about in her mind for some vet who might be suitable. No, Hastings was no good. He couldn't tell a lame horse from a gnu. Dr. Watoski was mostly cattle and sheep, and it took him forever to get to the ranch in an emergency. McCoy was O.K. but he charged the moon, never really talked with her about "his patients," just rushed in and out. She needed a vet who would treat her as an equal, or at least with respect. And she needed a competent veterinarian who could help her get her mare to the Tevis Cup race in sound condition. One minor health problem could keep her out of competition.

Rachel's thoughts were interrupted by a snort to her left, and she realized she had nearly walked into the black filly, Night Ember, who was tied in the aisle.

"Here's one that needs floating," she said, and headed for the tack room to get the vet list. She stared at the vacant place on the wall for some time before it dawned on her that Kate must have the list. Get a grip on yourself, she thought.

She returned to the barn aisle as they filed the sharp edges off the filly's teeth. There was Fred Stewart lounging on a hay bale. Kate—her earlobe-length blue-black hair falling free of the red bandanna, her high russet cheekbones rosy with excitement —held the filly. The fragile Eastern flower, with arms up to the elbow in the yearling's mouth, rasped away.

At least she's not afraid of horse spit, Rachel thought sulkily.

The afternoon wore on with Kate, Fred, and Dr. Carson chatting away in friendly tones as Rachel watched silently for some blunder from this female veterinarian being foisted off on her while reliable old Fred went off to enjoy himself in early retirement. Kate, on the other hand, thrilled that they would have this attractive, knowledgeable woman coming to the ranch, could not figure out what was eating Rachel.

As Kate turned out the last horse, Dr. Carson said to Rachel with a smile, "A remarkably fit and healthy group of horses you have here."

"Thanks. I breed them to be tough, and put a lot of miles on them. Do you ride, Dr. Carson?" Rachel added to be polite.

"Please call me Margaret. Yes, I do. Mostly dressage, but I have done some eventing."

"That's like in the Olympics?" interrupted Kate, her dark brown eyes already showing signs of adulation.

Margaret laughed. "Yes, but not nearly so good."

As they reached the jeep, Rachel said, "If you find yourself with time on your hands, you would be welcome to come out and ride. We could scare you up something to throw a saddle on." Believing Dr. Carson to be in for far more in this territory than she had figured on, Rachel felt safe in making the offer.

"Thanks, I might take you up on that. I sold my Thoroughbred before I came out here. Your Arabians look a lot smaller, but I guess they can carry me."

"I reckon they can, Dr. Carson."

On the way back to town, Margaret pumped Fred on the subject of Rachel Duncan. His monosyllabic replies, mined with much effort, only tantalized her more. Rachel had never married, she learned. Had run the ranch herself after her father's death. Occasionally had a young woman working for her. Was well respected in the small ranching community.

Her mind still on Rachel, Margaret said good-bye to Fred Stewart and climbed the stairs to her second-story apartment. This is a woman I would like to get to know, she thought, letting herself into the sunny rooms. "I am going to accept her not-too-enthusiastic offer," she announced, chuckling at herself as she picked up El Gordo, her fifteen-pound orange tailless cat.

All through dinner Rachel suffered Kate's bubbling enthusiasm about wonderful Dr. Carson. Finally, Kate left for the bunkhouse, allowing Rachel to sink down in peace in the softest chair she could find with a short glass of Irish whiskey. She thought back over the years that Dr. Stewart had cared for the ranch livestock, his reassuring presence making the hard times after her father's stroke more bearable. They had been rough years as she learned the management of the ranch, nearly too much for a girl of eighteen.

Her dad had been an early importer of Arabian horses from Poland after World War II. A few of his finest mares had gone into the country's best breeding programs. Rachel had shown the horses from the time she was quite small, filling a trophy room with ribbons and silver. She did it to please her father, though she hated almost every moment of it. The horses were treated like beauty queens: shaved, clipped, oiled, confined to preserve the gloss of coat, the length of mane and tail. They were encouraged to be "brilliant," but most were simply unmanageable.

Rachel was very annoyed with the preciousness of the way they were handled when she knew that they were sensible, hardy, and smart. When she was sixteen, just after her mother died, Rachel told her father she wouldn't show his horses anymore. It was as if she suddenly no longer cared to please him. He was never satisfied anyway. Her father understood, without any discussion, that he had lost her.

The day of Rachel's high school graduation, her father had a stroke. During the long years of caring for him, of dealing with his foreman, Jim, she looked for excuses to leave the ranch on her mare Erika. At the age when most teenage girls are discovering their freedom, Rachel felt suffocated. With her college money, carefully saved since childhood, she bought a herd of sixty Herefords. Keeping track of the cattle helped her keep her sanity. She rode out long hours. It was Dr. Stewart who had asked one day, "Don't you think you cover at least fifty miles some days with your mare?"

"'Course we do. Often enough."

Fred had looked at the unhappy teenager and knew she needed something that could be hers, something she could be good at without the imposition of her father's rigid standards. He told her about the Big Horn ride the following month near Billings. She had only vaguely heard of distance riding and was intrigued by the sport.

Rachel and Erika entered, and finished in third place. They would have been first if they hadn't gotten four penalty points for crossing the finish line early. It was fun. Rachel had a terrific time and decided this was the sport for her. From then on, she and Erika competed in every ride they could get to, and it had never soured on them.

Erika had eventually gone into the brood-mare band. Hard as it was to give up riding her, Rachel knew, for that very reason, it was important to breed her. Rachel had been right. Before Erika died at the age of thirty-one, she had mothered, nuzzled, and fussed over six splendid foals, and was grandmother to twenty-nine through her son, Distance Hawk. Rachel's best horse was now Erika's last daughter, Kestrel.

Rachel had selected the breeding stock, since her father's death, not just for beauty or championships collected or fad pedigree lines, but for endurance, strong clean conformation, and kind intelligence. Only occasionally was a mare kept back for the breeding herd. She had to be outstanding and especially good at her job—working cows or covering miles—a mare like Storm Queen or Kestrel.

Rachel kept a waiting list of people who wanted one of her horses. It being widely known that they were well broken and honestly described, whether they went to pleasure riders, serious working cowhands, or distance competitors, they always brought top dollar.

Rachel was glad she lived the way she did. Sometimes she tried to imagine herself at a city job, but it was a picture that wouldn't come into focus.

She looked out her bedroom window at the moonlit lodgepole pines. Throwing open the window, she was caught by the distinct, almost tangible, smell of lilacs. She let the dark night mixed with the aroma of the deep lavender flowers enfold her as she undressed for bed.

Two

Early morning dark in the sweet hay-scented barn, with the soft sounds of horses eating their breakfast, was the most soothing time of the day for Rachel. She liked to work alone around the horses or just sit quietly listening. Any human talk seemed like mindless chatter.

The brindle greyhound Woody leaned against her leg, reminding her to let him out. A track reject narrowly spared from destruction, Woody had found his place at the ranch—always an elegant gentleman, a playful companion, and not much of a watchdog. Perhaps he kept the rats from being too bold in the tack room. Rachel affectionately saw him out the door, checking while she was there for a light in the bunkhouse. *No, Kate wasn't up yet.*

She put Kestrel and Storm Queen on the cross-ties centered in the aisle, so she could work around them. With the hoof pick, she cleaned each foot and checked that the shoes were still nailed on tight. She went through the never-tiring ritual of grooming. First, the rubber curry comb used in massaging circular patterns to loosen the dirt and old hair. The stiff brush came next, stroking and flipping off the dirt. The soft body brush was her favorite part of grooming, following the whorls and changes in the hair pattern, sleeking the coat. The horses usually liked to have their faces brushed. Kestrel, especially, would bob her head when Rachel stopped brushing, bumping Rachel's arm until she did it some more.

Rachel leaned against Kestrel's warm body, face in her mane. She stroked the low cleft of the mare's chest as she spoke softly to her. "I don't know what to do. Fred has always been there. I never thought he wouldn't be." Standing back, she pulled a little snarl from the white mane. Rachel knew that many horses in training for the Tevis Cup didn't make it to the starting line. She was worried that an improperly treated training injury or health problem could be permanent.

"I couldn't bear it if anything happened to you." Rachel reached up to scratch the mare in the deep gully between her jaw bones. Kestrel's lips quivered with pleasure. When she felt her person lean quietly into her again, she rubbed her lips against Rachel's shoulder in a lupping way. Mutual grooming of old friends.

"What would Kate think if she saw us like this?" she tried to joke. "I'm turning into a sentimental cuss. Well, we've got our work cut out for us today, better get on with it." She headed for the tack room.

Today they would be riding to the small ranch her father had bought before she was born. Connected to the main ranch by a Bureau of Land Management-leased grazing range, and the Lewis and Clark National Forest, the small two-room log cabin, hay barn, and corrals were built near the spring that became the Judith River. Jim, her father's old ranch foreman, lived there and kept track of the two- and three-year-old horses. It was a good place for them to grow up sure-footed, tough, and independent —the foothills of the Little Belts ensured that. Jim grained them in long troughs during winter, and threw out hay. Once a month they were all rounded up for the blacksmith to trim their feet and to be dosed for worms. Other than that they had their freedom, an arrangement that suited Rachel just fine. She had never been happy with Jim's training methods, and this system was her way to make sure that the horses had a minimum of contact with him.

Rachel believed early handling stayed with a horse the rest of its life, so she kept the yearlings at the home ranch. She and Kate worked almost daily with each of them, teaching the basics: standing still to be handled, picking up their feet, being led anywhere, and traveling in the horse trailer. The fall of their yearling year, they were driven with a few steady older mares to the line ranch and given over to Jim's care until the spring of their fourth year.

This spring she and Kate would be driving back fourteen four-year-old horses ready for their higher education. They represented the main income for the ranch, and Rachel was curious to see how the recent winter had brought this year's bunch to full growth. She still remembered the day six years before when she had first seen the adult Kestrel and known she had a hundred-mile horse.

In the tack room she selected the saddles to fit the horses they would be riding, and snaffle bridles with long Western reins. The saddle blankets had been made by one of Kate's grandmother's friends, a Hopi woman who dyed and wove them of wool from her own small flock of sheep. Each had its own story in color and design. At first Rachel had balked at using them for everyday, but they had outlasted everything else and the horses' backs never got sore.

With the saddles in place and cinched up, Rachel had time to wonder again if Kate was awake and had made the lunch. She opened the door when she heard Woody's whine to be let back into the warm barn. The dark bunkhouse was only faintly visible in the predawn dark. Damn, she thought. Kate's not up yet. A sound next to her brought her hackles up until Kate's sleepy "Mornin' " made her realize the light had been on and off. Maybe a total of ten minutes. *Great.*

"What did you fix for lunch? Spaceburgers?"

Kate just laughed, her easy humor taking the edge off Rachel's grumps. "I made it last night. Don't worry, it's good."

"What?" Rachel asked suspiciously.

"Tamales, cut-up pears, apricots, and cucumbers—and to drink, lemons in water. Oh, and vanilla-filled chocolate cupcakes."

Rachel figured it would sound a lot better in five or six hours. Kate put the lunch in the saddlebags, and they slid the cinches tight, then led the horses into the moonless half-dawn. Mounted, they set off cross-country at a walk that lengthened as the horses warmed. Today would be a forty-mile round trip.

Looking east to the Big Snowy Mountains, Rachel could just

see the first glow of the sun glistening over the edges. She had not been aware until then of a general feeling of anxiety. It made her crabby and distracted.

Kate rode up next to her to ask, "What's wrong?"

Rachel looked at her in surprise. "Does it show? I'm not sure. . . ."

"You don't know?" Kate asked with genuine concern.

"I think I'm worried about that new vet. What if Kestrel runs into trouble and she can't handle it?"

"Why in blue blazes not?" Kate asked, puzzled.

When faced directly with this question, the only answer Rachel could come up with was that Margaret Carson was a woman. She blushed. She was too ashamed to say that.

"Let's shake the dust off these horses," she said, moving on up the trail at a brisk trot.

Ginger subject, Kate thought.

The sun was barely at the wide-hipped stage, before it slipped over the edge of the world, when they reached the high, rolling grasslands. With the inviting stretch of buffalo grass ahead, and the Big Snowies off to the left, their drainages still lined with snow, it was too much to refrain from a joyous gallop. Rachel's love of this country, shared fully with Kate, had a heady, boundless feeling that she knew must be like being in love. She had only felt that once for a person, a long time ago.

The canter loosened up the riders as well as the horses. Kate ventured, "Maybe you and Dr. Carson could get to know each other. You know, be friends?"

Rachel turned, baffled, and stared at her. "Why would we want to do that?"

Uncomfortable with direct questions, Kate answered round the point, "A woman your own age to be buddies with could be very good."

"I never think about it. I've got all the buds I want down at the Silver Saddle bar."

"I don't mean those guys you meet up with once every blue moon. I'm talking about. . .well, Sarah is real important to me. Even though she doesn't like horses, we still share a lot between us."

"Yes. Sometimes I feel real lonely, in a way the fellas at the bar don't fill." Rachel's eyes were unfocused, not moving along the rim of the horizon's mountains but resting on one small point of the line. She filled her lungs with a deep gulp of air, turned to Kate, and said, "I don't really have much time or inclination to dwell on that. Don't often wish I'd married." She gave a soft snort of a laugh. "In fact, damn rarely."

They stopped for lunch a mile or two from the line ranch, in a cool steep-walled canyon where the Judith River was just a stream. Rachel, watching the hobbled horses grazing nearby, revised her opinion of Kate's meal planning upward. The cool cucumbers and fruit were wonderful with the tamales.

Turning the last bend in the canyon they rode out onto the open flats. Rachel noticed with relief that the horses were all penned. Jim came out of the cabin as they rode up. He and Rachel looked over the four-year-olds, then walked over to the two- and three-year-olds, held in a separate pen so they couldn't follow them back to the main ranch. Jim repeated, word for word, his yearly advice on them, telling her, "In your father's day, I would have had these colts broke by now."

Rachel patiently said, "I like to do it different, Jim."

He pushed his old-fashioned Stetson to the back of his head, frowned, and scratched his perpetual day-old beard. Rachel had only seen him clean-shaven once, at her father's funeral. "It's a waste just lett'n them get away with do'n noth'n, eat'n their heads off. We had 'em broke and sold by the time you first throw a saddle on them."

"I don't like to ride them 'til they are full-grown. I think they stay sound all their lives if you give them time to grow first." She wished she could get through just one spring without having this conversation.

"Well, you're the boss." He turned back to the cabin. "Still got the same gal, I see."

"Yes. Kate."

He went up the stairs, saying over his shoulder, "Coffee's hot." Kate muttered, "Still."

They sat down to coffee so dark no amount of cream changed

its color, and politely refused some very dubious chili beans.

Jim always had to play the he-man part with the young women who worked the ranch. "What's your boyfriend's name?" he questioned Kate with a leer.

"Don't have one."

"Oh now, honey, ya better get started. Life's too short to go manless," he chuckled, thinking himself a candidate, no doubt.

"I've got a girlfriend," she flashed.

"Hell, that don't count."

"Wanna bet?" Kate said, slamming out the screen door.

Rachel gave a long look at the screen door as she picked up her gloves. "I'm going into Lewistown tomorrow. Do you have a grocery list?"

He pulled out a greasy piece of brown paper bag from the mess on the table and handed it to her. She never knew why they went through this ritual. His grocery list hadn't varied in twenty years.

"We better head those horses out. Thanks for the coffee." Rachel retrieved her hat from the back of her chair and settled it low over her eyes as she walked out the door. She found Kate waiting for her near the corral gate.

"Is he more disgusting than last year, or is it my imagination?"

Rachel hadn't seen Kate pissed very often. Her lips were pressed together, her eyes furious under her bangs and fluorescent pink baseball cap.

"Jim has stayed pretty much the same over the years. This line camp is not very productive with him here, but I promised my dad I would keep him on. And better here than at the home ranch." She looked at Kate with amusement. "He sure knows the way to get under your skin."

"Yuck, what a thought." Kate threw open the gate with spill-over vehemence.

Kate mounted up and drove the four-year-olds out of their pen, and Rachel led off, heading the bunch toward the northeast. Kate tailed, making sure none tried to turn around. The ride back seemed twice as fast, with Kestrel and Storm Queen eager for home and the young horses remembering, as they went, that they had been that way before.

A nice chestnut filly stood out from the herd. She traveled in an alert, self-confident way, spirited without being foolish. "That one might be a keeper," Rachel said, pointing her out.

"Yeah, isn't she nice? I've been watching her, too."

As Kate and Rachel drove the young horses, they were learning much that would influence how they would approach each individual animal when the time came to put a saddle to them.

A few miles from home, one of Stormy's shoes came loose. Kate jumped off. "What a drag. Couldn't the damn thing have waited half an hour?" She stared helplessly at the horseshoe twisted off to the side.

"Let's check the damage," Rachel said, reaching into her saddlebag and bringing out her tool pouch. First, she rasped off the nail clenches, then pulled the shoe all the way off with some combination wire cutters and shoe pullers. Dropping the bent shoe into the saddlebags along with her tool pouch, she said, "I think her foot will hold up all right until we get back," and swung back up into the saddle.

Kate was once again impressed with her employer's easy competency. She thought, I don't figure how she can be so good at everything she does yet have no faith this new vet knows what she's doing. Rachel Duncan is not acquainted with any woman her equal, and that's the truth and the trouble.

It was close to four o'clock when they rode through the gates at home. After sorting out the horses and doing chores, they headed for their respective baths and evenings—Kate to drive into Judith Gap to meet Sarah and stay overnight, Rachel to settle in with the latest Dick Francis mystery.

Before Rachel turned in at eight, she did her evening rounds, checking on the mares still due to foal. Sparrow Hawk was one of them. She had been bred to the Tevis Cup winner of three years before, and hers would be a foal with promise.

The mares looked up with mild interest, still munching their evening hay, as Rachel walked by the stall doors. It was a great setup, Rachel thought, pleased with the improvements she'd made on her father's design. The big foaling boxes each had one-acre corrals leading off, so the mares could come and go as they liked. They stayed there for two weeks after foaling, then joined the others in the broad valley pasture.

Sparrow Hawk seemed near to foaling. Her vulva was long and draping, the muscles soft as jelly on either side of her tail. Rachel looked closely at her udder. It was shiny and hard, but no sign yet of the waxy "candles" that push out ahead of the milk.

Rachel shut the bottom half of the corral's Dutch door. "I think we'll keep you in tonight, my dear," she said softly as she scratched the mare behind her ears and stroked her long, smooth chestnut neck.

Walking back up to the house, Rachel noticed the absence of lights from the bunkhouse. She felt a flash of loneliness before the stars found her and delighted her with their cheerful winking. Sliding under the sheets, she experienced a deep, delicious sensation of relief. Her body had been ready to quit hours ago, but her head had been too busy to pay attention.

Three

The shrill phone in the strange apartment woke Margaret from deep, sensuous dreaming. "Dr. Carson here," she murmured, drawing her reluctant wits about her.

"Rachel Duncan out in the valley."

Margaret's eyes snapped open; she looked at the clock. Two, it said.

"I've got a mare foaling in trouble. It's been ten minutes of seeing one front leg and I can't get hold of the other. McCoy's out of town. Better come quick."

"Try to keep her from straining and—"

"Yes, yes." Rachel's voice impatiently broke into Margaret's instructions, followed by a sharp plastic click.

As she jammed her hair up on her head with a large clip, Margaret tried to overcome her annoyance at being hung up on. "And second best to McCoy, for crying out loud," she said to El Gordo.

She yanked on coveralls over bare body, shot her feet into rubber boots, and raced for the door. Everything she might need was packed in the tool caddy of her Toyota truck. Pounding down the apartment stairs, she was suddenly aware of the racket she was making, but by that time the door had slammed with a resounding crash. How to win friends and influence people. She wouldn't last long in this building if there were many late-night calls.

She ignored the speed limit between Judith Gap and Buffalo. "It's a shame to waste all this nice paved road," she told her truck. But when the Toyota hit the corduroy of the dirt roads, complaints and warnings in Japanese threatened a breakdown or, at the least, bank-breaking repair bills. Reluctantly, Margaret slowed down.

"If this truck falls apart on the way, I won't be much help to the mare," she said reasonably, to herself. "As well as not presenting a very professional image." The image of her actual appearance flashed before her eyes: her rat's-nest hairdo, coveralls uncertainly buttoned. She wasn't even certain her boots were on the right feet. Laughter welled up, but behind the laughter lay the anxiety of knowing Rachel's lack of confidence in her, and that there was no way to get there quickly enough. She knew, too, that for Rachel, waiting while she watched her mare in pain, time was passing in a different dimension.

Tightening her grip on the steering wheel and calling on the white mare Epona, ancient Druid goddess of the horse, Margaret spoke softly, "Please, please, let this go all right."

Finally, far ahead she saw the lights of the ranch. The truck bounced over the cattle guard and before long roared up to the barn. Rachel was waiting with the door open. "I'm glad you're here."

Margaret knew it for an enormous understatement. As she opened the tool caddy of her truck and pulled out her bag, Rachel said, "The mare is getting tired. I've tried to keep her up and moving, but I can't anymore. There's hot water in a bucket. Need anything else?"

"No, lead the way." When Rachel turned to go back into the barn, Margaret got a quick look at her boots. Everything O.K. there. One of those potentially horrible giggles tried to escape, but Margaret caught it in time and changed it to a serious throat clearing. Rachel cast a glance back over her shoulder as she opened the stall door.

The sorrel mare raised her head and stood to see the stranger enter the stall. A good sign, Margaret thought. While she scrubbed as if for surgery, she watched the mare. The animal was breathing heavily, sweat running off her coat.

Rachel began a nervous history. "This is Sparrow Hawk. One of my best mares. She's up on all of her shots. Fourth foal. No trouble before." She anxiously tucked in her shirttail. "That's a well-bred foal in her. Hope it comes out alive." She took a deep breath. "I found myself awake and walked down to check on her. I heard the water break as I came up to the stall."

All nine hundred pounds of horse heaved to the straw, groaned, and tried to expel a reluctant foal. Sparrow Hawk rolled, thrashed her legs, banging her hooves against the wall, then was still. Rachel moved to make her rise.

"That's all right. I can examine her lying down." Margaret stretched out next to her and carefully slid her arm into the mare's vulva, feeling her way past the one leg just at the opening. The vaginal passage was dry now of amniotic fluid, long since released in the normal flow of things to make the delivery of the foal easier. Wasted. Her hand came to the foal's chest and found the head folded back with the other front leg. "Sweet Epona, no," she muttered into the straw. Visions of textbook fetalectomies flashed through her mind. She rebelled at the thought of a foal lying sectioned on the floor after eleven months of growing.

"Come on, baby," Margaret hissed through clenched teeth, straining against the efforts of the mare to push her foal out. Her mind was silently racing. *Probably dead. Damn the odds.* Her arm muscles gave up then, no match for the equine system designed to send a sixty-pound baby to the air in fifteen carefree minutes.

Margaret lay there for a minute, letting the feeling come back into her numb arm. Fighting to keep emotion off her face, she unbuttoned her coveralls and slid her right arm out of the sleeve, totally unmindful that her exposed breast was shining like a full moon. Out of her kit, she dug a rope with a small noose at one end and dunked it in the disinfectant bucket as she resoaped her arm.

"Is it alive?"

"I don't know yet."

Margaret lay back in the straw, dug her boots into the wall, and passed the rope into the desolate channel. She crept past the leg, the chest, the throat, and could just reach the muzzle. If she could slip the loop over the lower jaw, there might be a chance of getting the head around. Her finger reached in the mouth to pry the jaw open, and she felt her finger licked! She would have danced if her arm had not been encased in horse. At that moment, a violent contraction neatly expelled her arm, and the mare struggled to rise. Margaret decided it was time to get up too.

"It's alive. There's a chance if. . ." If we can get it out soon and in one piece, she finished silently. She applied herself to vigorously resoaping her arm. Rachel, even with her concern about the mare, tried hard not to look at Margaret's breast. Sparrow Hawk took a few staggering steps, switched her tail, then crashed back down to the straw.

"Easy, baby, easy," Margaret crooned. She lay down again, her escaped hair mixing with the honey color of the mare's tail, both blending into the gold of the straw. "Just let me come into you." When the contractions ended, she plunged deep into the mare, searching for that tiny muzzle holding such promise. This time, her fingers seemed to slip easily to the jaw and around the tiny teeth. Did the mare know, or was she past trying to deliver her foal?

"Here," Margaret cried to Rachel, "hold this rope and keep a steady pressure on it. Don't pull until I tell you." Pushing the foal's chest, she reached deeper to grasp the other tiny hoof and pull it forward, straightening the leg that had been bent back. "Now steady. . .even. . .not too hard," Margaret chanted as she pushed the foal's chest deep into the uterus. She could feel the head start to come around very slowly, then rest between the legs.

In one great expulsive surge, as if the mare knew it was time, the foal was released from its life-support system turned prison.

The foal looked dead lying there. Margaret grabbed the head, cleared the nostrils and blew into them, then lifted the hindquarters and gave a little shake. There was a small wheeze. Rachel's strong hands dragged the foal around to the mare's head. Sparrow Hawk's body rumbled a deep whickering welcome. The foal raised its head and answered with a squeak.

At this point, Margaret thought, the mare's nuzzling and whuffling will do more than medical science can for this foal. Her strength no longer needed, draining from her, Margaret lay spent in the straw.

Rachel lifted the tail for an unabashed look at the genitals. "A filly!" she cried.

Margaret didn't care. She smiled and watched the pulse of the umbilical cord lessen, knowing the time was coming when it would be safe to break it. The first home-leaving complete. She reached out one gentle hand to hold a small hoof with its soft yellow protective pad that would soon fall off to leave the hoof sharp and hard.

Rachel, aware that she was the only one standing, moved around to sit next to the wall. Margaret scooted back to join her. They grinned at each other. It would be close to an hour's show, the filly's struggle to stand and nurse the vital first milk full of antibody-rich colostrum.

The filly raised her wobbly head and lurched in her first effort to stand. Margaret rolled over to her bag, got out the iodine bottle, and doused the end of the stump where the cord had just broken.

This was a time not to interfere, the bonding time of mare and foal. Sparrow Hawk, exhausted, lay watching her new creation with galvanized fascination. She kept singing a low rumbling lullaby to her baby, who, with wet wavering head, was trying to get her bearings in this suddenly boundless, gravity-defined world. The filly shook her head, put one leg in front, jerked her hind legs, and nosedived to the straw.

The humans laughed with compassion. "It's always so new," Rachel said. "A miracle."

"Yes. I can tell you now I didn't think we would be watching this."

Both women, sobered, looked at each other. There was a new respect in Rachel's eyes. She saw sitting beside her a tired, competent woman veterinarian. She also saw the bared Amazonian breast with the shucked sleeve of the coveralls wet and crumpled in the straw. A deep scarlet rose over Rachel's face.

"You must be cold. I'll get you something to wear and put the kettle on."

"Oh good. I'd like some coffee."

Feeling extremely awkward and trying very hard to keep her eyes out of the vicinity of Margaret's chest, Rachel blurted out,

"I meant for a bran mash. For the mare." She opened the stall door. "But I can make some coffee too." She bolted out the door.

A slow smile crept over Margaret's face. She could hear the rattle of the grain bin opening, the flump of bran going into the bucket, and a few questioning neighs from horses wondering if it were early breakfast time. A few moments later, a sweatshirt dropped down next to her. She gratefully put it on to the sound of Rachel's steps retreating down the barn aisle.

"What is the story of your rancher?" Margaret asked the mare. "Is she a traveler from Lesbos? Perhaps you would know, being an expatriate of Arabia. The Fertile Crescent and all." She giggled. Watch yourself, she thought. You're being silly. Get serious. Even if the woman blushes like a cardinal every time she sees a usually covered body part, that does not mean she has sexual feelings. Could be a prude. Dear me, what chance would anyone have to be a lesbian in such isolated country, anyway? Well, be honest, isn't that why you came here?

Flashing back on the pain and discouragement of one too many failed relationships, Margaret reminded herself that she had come to terms with dreams versus reality. The reality was that being single allowed her to lead a calm, stable life, and that at times she was fairly happy. El Gordo's simple warm body pressed against hers at night was all the bed company she wanted.

Trudy had been the last straw. It was two years since Margaret's deadening discovery that she was once again being lied to about a secret affair. And once again Trudy's victim had been one of Margaret's friends, a double betrayal whittling away her circle of support, destroying trust. She knew she had further isolated herself, pushing away friends to try to control the "substance" Trudy was addicted to.

She finally had understood that she loved a woman who rode on the high of the initial love/sex encounter, especially if it were secret. Margaret thought Trudy could change. Probably Trudy *could* change, but not in time to meet Margaret's needs. Margaret's self-respect eroded, her body shut down. She became numb.

Trudy's last fling made it possible to leave her. Margaret could no longer be part of the dance. She didn't feel much like dancing. Her body's joy had flown along with her sexuality. At thirty-eight, she was emotionally worn-out and ready for a change, a new start away from everyone she had known and all the incestuous connections.

"So what are you worried about?" she asked herself. Heterosexual women had always been off-limits for her.

Rachel returned with a steaming bucket of mash and two cups of coffee. The wonderful combination of aromas filled the stall.

"Reminds me of hot breakfasts of Wheatena when I was a kid," Margaret told Rachel. She thanked her for the coffee, and they both settled in to watch the foal.

"Have you a name yet?" Margaret asked.

"I'd thought of Dawn Falcon just now when I was in the kitchen. It's not the name I'd planned, but I like it better. What do you think? You should have a hand in this." She smiled at Margaret, mostly with her eyes.

Margaret felt a tiny rush, then fixed her mind on the subject at hand, which was trying to stand. "I like it."

"I name Erika's line after birds. Sparrow Hawk is a full sister to Kestrel, the mare I'm training for the Tevis Cup."

"Oh." The specialness of this mare came home to Margaret.

The filly made another burst of effort, legs crossed, pointing in all directions, none directly under herself, but she was standing.

"Look, Dawn is rising," Rachel quipped. They both laughed, Rachel surprised at herself for making a joke.

Dawn, baffled about what to do next with these four things under her, tried to take a step. Crash. The mare, perhaps to set a good example, rose to her feet. She swayed slightly but looked surprisingly good after her ordeal. She nuzzled the filly, gently licking her back.

Dawn burst straight up, this time with all four legs directly beneath her, and shuffled close to the mare. She started sucking on the mare's knee, bumping and burrowing under the chest, hunting for the nipple. The mare, an old hand at this, moved forward and stretched her near hind leg back to make it easy for the filly to find the right place. Milk was streaming in two yellowish-white cascades. After much butting and many reeling misses, the satisfied slurping sounds told Margaret and Rachel that contact had finally been made. It seemed like a short drink for so much effort when the filly dropped to the straw like a stone and was instantly asleep. The mare carefully lay back down, rolled to her side, and with a few more contractions passed the placenta.

Margaret and Rachel rose, picked up the slimy mass, and carried it out of the stall. Together, they spread it out to make sure it was all there, nothing torn off and left inside to cause an infection. It was lovely, this eleven-month home of the filly. Like a spaceship. It was a soft blue-grey, shiny with veins emptied now of blood into the foal, a tree of life leading down into the umbilical cord. Turning it inside out, they carefully examined the velvety cushion, red and plush, that was the attachment to the mare's uterus.

"Looks good," Margaret said. "They've both come through this very well. I'll just give the filly a tetanus shot before I go."

"Would you like to have breakfast at the house? We can come back down here to do that before you leave, if you want."

"Yes, I'd like that." As Margaret leaned over to pick up her bag, she felt the stiff dry sleeve bump her leg. "I'm a mess," she laughed. "Look at me. Are you sure you want me in the house?"

"My house isn't a stranger to blood and muck. I'll find some fresh clothes for you, and you can take a bath if you like."

As they walked up to the house, there was a fine line of pink to the east.

Emerging from the hot soothing bath, Margaret saw a turtleneck and sweatpants laid out on the bed. A pair of socks and slippers were on the rug below them. When she came into the kitchen, she was met by Rachel, who herded her into the low-ceilinged living room to a deep chair. On the small table next to her were a steaming cup of coffee and two small white jugs of sugar and cream, the cream thick and yellow, straight from the cow's living body.

"My, my, this is service," she called out to Rachel, busy in the kitchen. She settled deep into the chair, aware of her trembling muscles, and looked out the window to the sky glowing peach and yellow.

Minutes later, Margaret woke with a jerk, immediately wondering if she had been drooling. Rachel was standing over her, telling her breakfast was ready.

Margaret was well into the grapefruit before she had her wits about her. The grapefruit had been neatly sectioned. Nobody had done that for her since she was three. Before her stood a hot bowl of Wheatena.

"Thought you'd like a bran mash, too," Rachel drawled across to her.

Margaret's blue eyes glowed. "Quite a spread, as you say out here." She poured thick cream and maple syrup over her cereal and dug in. "Where's Kate?" she asked.

"In town, staying over with a friend." Rachel's hand smoothed the worn oilcloth, the checked pattern long ago erased. She felt a tense excitement and a close ease that she did not understand. She looked across the table at Margaret scraping her bowl. An extraordinary woman, she thought. Like none I've met before. Maybe Kate is right. . . . It might be fun to get to know her.

Margaret, meanwhile, was vowing to keep her distance. It was true she felt drawn to Rachel, but, she told herself firmly, she did not need to get romantically involved with some virgin rancher who was probably homophobic as hell.

Rachel, refilling both of the coffee cups, said, "I've been thinking which horse you might like to ride. There's a six-year-old gelding might make a good jumper, or, uh. . . hunter. I'd like to know what you think of him."

In spite of Margaret's vow to distance herself from the Duncan spread, she found herself nibbling like a trout. "Is this one of the Arabs?"

"He's a cross-bred experiment. I tried some Thoroughbred-Arabian crosses, but they all ended up like Winnie the Pooh, very little brain. So I tried a Cleveland Bay stallion from Connecticut." At Margaret's raised eyebrows, she explained further. "Flew the semen out here to artificially inseminate the mare. That's why I call him Fly Up. You can take a look at him when we go out to the barn."

Margaret had always liked the big English horses. Cleveland Bay was an old breed developed for fox hunting, using a blend of Thoroughbred, Arabian, and draft horse. They tended to run eighteen hands, a foot taller than a large Arabian, and to have a kind, solid presence.

"Tuesday I have some time in the morning," Margaret said. "Would that be all right?"

"I'll be around." Brown-green eyes with rays of wrinkles around them smiled their pleasure. "I'll give you a tour of the place."

Here I am, Margaret thought, a lemming headed for the cliff.

She rose to follow Rachel out the door. "Wait, I've got your slippers on." Margaret went back into the bathroom, collected her scummy overalls, found her boots by the door, and walked with Rachel into the morning. Rachel handed her a jeans jacket off a peg on the porch and took down a windbreaker for herself.

They stood side by side for a few moments. The smell of sage rode the wind lightly in and out of recognition. The thought registered somewhere in Rachel's inner brain that it must have rained lightly in the night. There was a change and freshness to the air. She felt very tired, yet at peace.

They paused outside Sparrow Hawk's birthing chamber to watch. Margaret rested her arms on the top of the stall door, her chin on her wrists. Rachel stood back a bit so she could look at Margaret as well as the new filly.

Dawn was up and nursing, mostly at the right spot. When she finished, she shook her head, gave a sound between a snort and a squeak, then tried a crow hop. Not quite coordinated enough for that maneuver, she tripped herself. She bounced up again, gazing around at her horizons.

"Might as well get it over with," Rachel said, going into the stall to wrap her arms around the baby's chest and rump. Margaret filled a needle, slid it into the filly's neck, and the deed was done.

"Aren't you going to give any antibiotics?" Rachel asked. "Dr. Stewart always did."

Oh dear, Margaret thought, direct comparison time. "I don't like to give routine antibiotics. One shot doesn't do much good, anyway." Except make the mare owner feel better, she continued in her mind. "The recovery of the mare and foal is excellent, and your stall is as fresh and clean as a hospital delivery room." She laughed, looking around at the well-banked new straw, the scrubbed walls, cobweb-free. "I don't foresee any problems with these two." She patted the mare on the neck. "She cleaned up her bran mash, didn't she?"

Rachel checked the polished bucket. "And then some." She gave Margaret a long look. "O.K. If you don't see the need, I'll accept that."

"Believe me, if I feel any animal needs antibiotics, I give them." Margaret put away her gear, and they watched the foal until she fell asleep in a heap of tangled legs.

As they turned to leave Margaret asked, "Aren't you going to blanket the mare?"

"Blanket her? Hell, no. It's summer."

Touché, Margaret thought. Looking at the mare, she admitted to herself that even though in any eastern stable the mare would be blanketed under these circumstances, Sparrow Hawk really did look just fine. Different customs, as the Greeks must have thought in Rome.

Rachel led the way out to the back corrals, put her foot on a lower rail, and said, "Here's the horse."

A big horse, just under sixteen hands, moved out from under the trees and up to the two women with a square, ground-covering trot. His coat was a deep red bay, in sharp contrast to his black points; and he carried no white markings to distract the eye from the richness of his color. His eyes were large and dark with a hint of royal purple, the ears small and alertly expressive. Margaret was impressed. Legs straight, cannon bones short, but the best thing was the way he moved. A true athlete, she thought. He came up to her and whuffled in her hair, getting the smell with a kindness that came out of every pore.

"Yes, I'll be here Tuesday. I wouldn't pass up a chance to ride this horse."

Four

K ate used the right rein of Storm Queen's bridle to ask her to move to the right. At the same time she closed her left leg so that the mare would move sideways. "Now, if you will take one more step, I can reach the mailbox," Kate said in a reasonable voice.

Each horse on the ranch was taught to move in any direction asked, toward or away from anything, no matter how frightening—or attractive. In the East it was called leg yielding and associated with dressage; here it was expected of every working cow horse.

The mail was often Kate's end goal on her rides. Usually there would be a letter from Sarah, which she could pocket away so it wouldn't be obvious to Rachel how many came. For that added air of romance, Kate read these steamy missives by candlelight. Often more than once. There were poems in the envelopes that had never seen the inside of a high school English Lit classroom.

There were times she wished Rachel was aware of her special relationship with Sarah. On the other hand, Kate had no idea what Rachel would feel about her if she knew that she was lovers with a woman. She did know that she dreaded having to cope with that moment.

"Stormy, you must stand still. This mailbox does not contain a monster. Today is the big day you get to see it opened."

Kate kept up a soft crooning conversation as she leaned over, tapped the metal box lightly, then opened the door. Storm Queen snorted and instantly made a two-pace leap to the left. Kate asked firmly for a return, and the mare obligingly minced over to the hated box. What is it about horses and mailboxes? Kate asked herself, reaching in to gather the mail. Three letters, one toothpaste sample, and the *Stockman's Journal*. The door squeaked shut without a repeat of the horse's gymnastics.

"Great. What a good girl." Kate continued her lavish praise while she flipped through the envelopes until she came to the one with blue ink, strong flowing script, and S.W.A.K. on the back. "Oh, dear." Kate blushed and stuffed the incriminating evidence deep in her jeans pocket.

At the barn she threw the reins over the hitching rail and took out a stethoscope to listen and count the mare's heartbeats. After fifteen seconds she multiplied by four. "Ah, pulse forty-four. You're getting fit, my sweet." She loosened the cinch and led the mare in long slow circles to do the final cooling out.

Rachel, coming back from town, backed the Chevy truck up to the barn and called out the truck window, "I got a large pizza with green pepper and black olives. You want to have dinner with me?"

"Awesome. Just a sec, I'll help unload the feed."

Kate pulled the saddle from Stormy, then ran her hand softly over the mare's back, feeling for cold or dry spots showing uneven saddle pressure. The sweat was even and warm. She lightly massaged Stormy's back, gave her water without letting her tank up, then turned her out in a nearby corral for the mare to finish her massage in the soft dirt. Grunts of pleasure reached Kate's ears as she walked back toward the truck. It had been a long hard ride today. Kate would check Stormy later, before she turned the mare out with her friends.

Together, Rachel and Kate made short work of unloading the hundred-pound bags of oats, corn, and bran. "You'd think I buy enough of this stuff that they would deliver," Rachel said. "I think it gets heavier every year. But," she added with a slow smile, standing back to watch Kate heft a bag of corn to her shoulder, "you're a damned sight prettier than those spitt'n, belching Neanderthalers working for Western Fargo Grain."

Kate had to duck to hide her expression. "Does she know what she's saying?" Kate whispered to herself on the way to the grain bin. On the way back, she stopped at the tack room for the saddlebags.

"I saw you had already picked up the mail. Anything interesting?"

Kate blushed totally red. "I dunno. Here it is." She thrust the saddlebags at Rachel, picked up two bags of groceries out of the truck, and stomped off to the house. Rachel threw the saddlebags over her shoulder, picked up the pizza, and followed, wondering at Kate's moodiness.

When the last of the purchases from town was put away, Kate slipped out the door, mumbling something about going to the bunkhouse to wash up. Rachel put the pizza in the oven and the beers in the freezer. Sitting down at the kitchen table, she shed her city boots, put her feet up on a chair to air, and opened the mail bag.

"Brush your teeth whiter than white," she read. "Hmm. Probably tastes like candy. Looks like a candy cane. . . maybe Kate wants it."

She pulled out the letters. A bill from Mike's Garage for truck repairs and a month's worth of gas. The Western States Trail Foundation. "This is it." Her feet came to the floor with the front legs of the chair. She tore open the envelope as Kate walked in.

"Wishes to inform you. . . Kate, I'm in. Kestrel and I are entered, we're going for the Tevis Cup." They stood, the big round table between them, grinning like fools at each other.

"But I thought you had sent in your entry months ago," Kate said."

"Yes, I did, but not everybody gets in. Some are put on a waiting list. I better go over Kestrel's training and competition schedule to make sure she peaks just before the ride." Reaching for the clipboard and calendar, Rachel put a large red *R* on the Tevis Cup date and started counting backward. Shoeing appointments, conditioning schedule, and length of rides were all figured months in advance of an important ride.

The smell of burning cardboard reached both women at the same moment, but only Kate reacted. Grabbing the box from the oven, she patted out the flames with a towel and dubiously opened the lid. The pizza was miraculously unscathed. She lifted it out and placed it on the table.

Rachel got the beers from the freezer and cracked the lids, saying, "I never could understand why people like sweet pop with their food."

"Different tastes," Kate shrugged. "What horses do you want brought along as back-up for Kestrel?"

Rachel picked up a slice of pizza and squinted as she bit off a long rope of cheese that wouldn't be separated from its parent. "I think we'll go along as we have been," she said eventually. "Kestrel is the first horse I've bred who could handle that grueling trail in winning time. Storm Queen could complete it in twenty-four hours, but it would be punishing her. She's only six—next year she could handle it." Rachel reattacked the pizza as she looked at Kate. "There really isn't a back-up."

"If we're going to do a lot of hauling in the next few months," Kate said, "you'll need to get a new tire for the left side of the trailer. That running light is on vacation, too. Remember? I'd like to make that Big Horn ride out of Billings. I could go see my father's family." Kate squirmed with energy in her chair. Rachel was delighted with her enthusiasm and realized again how she valued Kate's love of horses, her special sense of them.

"Yes, I've got you entered on Stormy. Kestrel will also be in that one. It's so close that Betty would only need to be here one night." Betty Dorset, an old high school friend of Rachel's and a reliable horsewoman, cared for the ranch when Kate and Rachel both had to be away.

They munched in silence for a while, each with her own thoughts. "Shall I take Fly Up out tomorrow?" Kate asked.

For some reason, Rachel felt awkward about answering. "Dr. Carson is going to ride him tomorrow. I'm interested in her opinion on his future as a jumping horse."

Kate looked closely at her and said in a neutral tone, "Oh."

"Those four-year-olds we brought up last week could take some sorting out."

"O.K., I'll get started on them."

"Watch that sorrel filly out of Changer. She has a skittish look and sulky ears."

"Sometimes that edge just makes me want to try harder to

win them over," Kate confessed. "Gentle her up and have her whinny when she sees me."

"You are an odd one, Miss Singer." Shaking her head, Rachel looked with affection at this woman half her age. "The Bitterroot fifty-mile is in three weeks. Kestrel's going, and since I've decided to sell Grey Crow, I figured it's time people see him. If you can just finish clean in a respectable time that will be enough. I've been pleased with him on the training rides we've done, so it's time for him to move on."

"I'll shake him out over the next couple of weeks and get to know him well. You say Dr. Carson's coming out?"

"Morning sometime." Rachel stood, dumped the cardboard in the trash and the bottles in the recycle bin. She felt keyed up. Well, of course I am, she thought. There's a lot to do between now and the Tevis Cup.

Kate got up. "Guess I'll turn in. I'm really glad you got into the Tevis Cup. I hope you'll let me crew for you. Lots I could learn. And, you know, anything I can do to help you. . .well, just tell me, O.K.?"

Rachel smiled at her, grateful for this awkward offer.

"Partners."

"Yeah. 'Night."

Five

The roar of the old vacuum cleaner in the dark morning air sounded incongruous to Kate as she walked from the bunkhouse to the barn. She stopped with her hand on the latch, a smile spreading broadly over her face. "Ah, yes. Dr. Carson is coming out for a social call." She pulled the handle to a chorus of welcoming neighs, unlatched the feed bin, and started mixing rations. Woody crept out of his blankets and stretched after the hard work of chasing dream rats.

First she grained the horses that would be worked that morning. She fed the mares, then refilled the foals' creep feeder. "Here you are, you little creeps." The seven babies scampered up to their twenty-four-hour grain feeding station, a little covered pen with narrow entries placed all around it so that the foals could come in to eat grain but the mares could only stand outside and drool.

Sparrow Hawk nickered politely when Kate entered the stall with her grain, but the new filly bucked and reared, butting her dam hard to get her to let down her milk. "Impatient greedy little pig," Kate said affectionately. "I sure am glad you are here in the world."

After the barn lights were turned off, she saw the pale grey light in the sky. She could no longer hear the vacuum cleaner but could smell bacon and coffee. She exchanged her saunter for a stride.

There was a rosiness to the house with the lights on this early, a warmth that spoke of home. Mindful of Rachel's cleaning binge, Kate shucked her tennis shoes at the door. The slate floor was scrubbed. The big round oak table glowed, freshly waxed, without its ratty oilcloth cover. There were no bridle bits soaking in the sink or pieces of leather lying on the counters.

Kate turned the bacon and poured herself some coffee. Carrying her mug, she explored further. She trod across the ancient frayed Oriental rug that covered most of the floor of the long, low-ceilinged living room. The one sofa sat in front of the fireplace, its russet corduroy covers dog and cat hairless, pillows plumped. The mantel of the fireplace was uncluttered, a single vase of fresh-cut lilacs at one end.

Kate loved the fireplace built from round stones. It reminded her of a photograph in her world history book of the many-breasted goddess Minerva.

Rachel's favorite chair had one of the new saddle blankets thrown over the back to hide the worn and puppy-chewed spots. Even the old photographs on the wall had been dusted. Kate looked at them. Rachel's father, Leslie Duncan, winning the Western Breeder's Cup thirty years before. Did he look happy or proud with the trophy in his arms, standing by his best mare? She peered into the indistinct eyes, looking for some clue to Rachel. His jaw seemed clenched shut, as if unable to show any pleasure. Kate wondered if he ever showed Rachel any of his pride in her. He must have felt it; she always reached for the best in herself.

Rachel was nearby in a small mahogany frame, a little girl on her fat Welsh pony, Thunder. When Rachel's parents stopped loving each other, Thunder took all of Rachel's sadness and confusion into her small chestnut body. And there was the photograph of Mildred, Rachel's mother, at her coming-out party the year before she entered Sarah Lawrence. Tall, composed, hair in a soft, low bun, wearing one of those narrow white lace-edged dresses that fairly screamed elegance and wealth. The eyes, Kate could see, were almost fierce. Her chin was up about an inch above what was necessary to project pride. She had brought down her family's wrath when she dropped out of college to marry a cowboy, as they called him. Kate studied the picture she knew was Rachel's favorite one of Mildred. Wearing a flower-print housedress with a full white apron over it, she squatted in the dust of the stable yard, smiling as she petted her dog Scout. These photographs, daily passed, were rarely actually seen. Kate found Rachel in the bathroom, cleaning the toilet. "Hey, is the Queen coming or something?"

Rachel rose to her feet, opened the cabinet under the sink, and chucked in the sponge and scouring powder. She grinned at herself as she said, "The stalls were looking cleaner. I had trouble sleeping past three, so I thought I'd give you something to rib me about. Why don't you make yourself useful and scramble some eggs? I'm almost done."

During breakfast the radio kept up a steady drumming as they half-listened for the six o'clock weather forecast and talked over the week's plans. Kate reminded Rachel that Sarah would be visiting Saturday and asked if she could hitch Nanna to the cart so they could go off for a picnic. "Sarah is so scared of horses, but I thought she might be able to handle riding in a cart."

"Sure, Nanna could use the exercise," Rachel said as she turned off the radio, somewhere in her inner brain having registered "clear, light wind from the southwest, chance of heavy rain in the long-range forecast."

Rachel walked out to the porch and felt alive: that sweet feeling of full awareness of breath moving in, of chest swelling, the elusive hint of sage, of horse. She was an integral part of all this. Her scent going to the horses, their manure going to the apple trees. In time her ashes going to the sage. It made her feel aligned.

She reached for her chaps, slipped them off their peg, and went through the dance of putting them on. On the inside of her legs, the suede was worn to a high gloss between her knee and lower calf. She buttoned her jeans jacket aged to a soft sky-blue in sharp contrast to the red polo shirt under it. The scent of Margaret came to her, lingering on the jacket. She raised the lapel to her nose, softly taking it in, and then gave a little leap, the Western high-heeled boots resounding off the boards.

As usual, Kate came out, letting the screen door slam, and skimmed over the boards in her tennis shoes. "You're looking frisky," she said. "I feel like this is going to be a wonderful day."

Rachel looked at her and felt that kind of smile that starts in the inner tense places and moves out to soft fingernails and hair roots. "It's unusual, at least. It'll be a first for pleasure riding with a vet. I hope she can handle this rough country. It's a lot different from tractor-leveled riding rings."

Margaret found them in the tack room going over shoeing charts and a miscellany of record keeping. Rachel looked up, pleased to see her. "So you weren't kept away by your calling?"

"No, I wouldn't mind being busier, as a matter of fact. What tack do you want me to use on Fly Up?"

"Usually we use stock saddles. You could try this Australian stock saddle. It's sort of a cross between English and Western." Rachel lifted it down from one of the higher racks and blew off the dust. "Not one of our more popular saddles, but it's comfortable and fits him well." Rachel handed Margaret a snaffle bridle. "He will neck rein or go on a direct rein."

Rachel took down Kestrel's bridle and swung her battered cutdown stock saddle over her right shoulder, hand hooked in the space under the horn, the underbelly of the saddle hanging over her shoulder like a gutted deer. She went out the door and down the aisle leading to the back corrals. Margaret stuck her head out the tack room door and watched Rachel's easy sauntering gracefulness. She looked back in at Kate.

Kate winked at Margaret. "You're supposed to follow her," she said with a wry grin.

A flash of recognition passed between them. Then Margaret put the bridle over her shoulder and picked up the Australian saddle the same way she carried her English saddle, over her arms. That lasted four steps' worth of stirrups, cinch, and fenders banging against her legs. She tried to sling the unwieldy thing to her shoulder but couldn't get the puzzle to fit. Still wrestling, she finally made it to where Rachel waited with a highly amused expression on her face.

"Takes some practice," she said. "Just give it a rest on the hitching rail." She indicated a stout bar supported by two posts about waist height. Margaret, with great relief, set her saddle next to Rachel's.

Fly Up ambled over to greet them. A white flash through the rails caught Margaret's eye, and she peered around the bay horse to see what it was.

"That's Kestrel," Rachel told her.

Margaret watched the white mare run across the corral. For the space of a few strides, their spirits were interwoven. Kestrel reached the rocks in the corner and bounded over them, mane and forelock falling over her face around small alert ears. Her tail flagged high, following her like a banner. This animal was the most sure-footed, coordinated athlete Margaret had ever seen, with a beauty that made her wonder how she could be worked as a beast of burden. Putting a saddle on this mare was akin to putting a jess on a hawk.

Rachel whistled to call Kestrel over, enjoying the impact she was having on Margaret. The mare came toward them at a trot to make an Olympic Grand Prix horse envious. She put her pretty little ears flat back at the bay gelding to assert her dominance and ownership of Rachel, and he gave way at a respectful distance.

Close up, Margaret could see that Kestrel was what is called a milk-white phase of grey. The black skin under the pure white hair was characteristic of Arabians and gave the coat a special glow.

Her large dark eyes studied Margaret with an intelligent curiosity and playfulness. Once again, Margaret felt a strange mixing of spirit boundaries. Taking a step back, she tried to unmerge.

"She is lovely. This is the horse you are doing the Tevis Cup on?"

"Yes."

Margaret studied Rachel's face for a sign that she was putting her on. She found none. She looked back at the horse, saw every tendon in the legs defined, the muscles long and flat with the veins like standing rivers just under the skin's thin surface.

"A hundred miles in one day?"

"More like ten to twelve hours if you're a winner."

"I guess I never realized they traveled so fast. Seems like a terrible hardship."

"Of course it is if horse and rider aren't fit. Veterinarians and teams of workers keep checking the horses. Half of the entries don't finish; either the vets pull them or the riders have enough sense to drop out. A lot of horses in training for it don't even reach the starting line." Rachel looked at Margaret. "That's where you come in—helping me reach the starting line."

Margaret saw in the tough horsewoman's face how important this challenge was to her and understood why it threw her to have a change in veterinarians. "I'll do my best," she said with her eyes on her patient, in the pink of health.

Rachel opened the gate and held up the bridle. Kestrel came up, lowered her head, and took the bit while her person lifted the headstall to rest behind her ears. Rachel snorted, "This cayuse practically puts on her own bridle. Must like something about this sagebrush hopping."

Margaret was impressed. Kestrel looked like a horse who likes what she's doing. Fly Up was a trifle more restrained but still the easiest horse she had ever put a bridle to. She noticed the big horse's shoes neatly done with clips pulled and set hot. "You have yourself a good farrier. I didn't expect to see such nice work out here."

"Yes, I know I'm lucky. Have to wait on him hand and foot," Rachel said, eyes shining with mischief. "His favorite bribe is Kate's tamales. All we have to do to get him to come out for a lost shoe or an emergency reset is say 'tamales' and he finds a place in his schedule." She placed the saddle gently on Kestrel's back and looked over the horn with a wonderfully playful expression.

When Margaret had Fly Up saddled, she led him out of the gate after Kestrel. He stood rock-still for her to mount. She had never before encountered such basic manners.

"How long are you up for spending in the saddle?" Rachel asked.

"I have all morning," Margaret answered, not really thinking. In Rachel's mind that rapidly computed to twenty miles at a six-mile-per-hour rate of fairly leisurely travel.

Kestrel set off on a limber, long-strided walk that matched most horses' trot speed. Margaret found she had to trot her horse occasionally just to keep up. Out of the valley they climbed, and as soon as they reached the crest of the ridge, Rachel set off at a fluid trot. They wound down through rocks and over terrain that Margaret, without a doubt, would have slowed to a walk to negotiate if she had not been with Rachel. Fly Up watched where he put his feet and didn't once stumble. Margaret began to feel confidence in his ability to manage the rough going. The rhythm of his stride and what she felt to be his intelligent, calm approach to this challenging footing were beginning to hold her interest. "I would like to see this horse handle a jumping course," she said.

"Sure thing," Rachel responded. She brought Kestrel to a halt and pointed off to the west. "You can just see the Big Belts and Mount Edith from here." There they were, with the morning's sun rolling over their rounded tops. "Look," Rachel said, indicating a small valley off to their right. "Wapiti."

Margaret saw a herd of maybe twelve reddish-brown deer-like animals. "Aren't they elk?"

"Yes, but they don't answer to either name. Wapiti is their old name."

As they rode down toward the herd, the cows gave their high-pitched warning squeal, turning the calves away, their yellow rumps flashing. The women rode on through the valley, the elk moving up into a fringe of pines as the invaders passed. After at least three miles of steady trotting, Margaret thought, Don't these horses ever walk? She cantered up to Rachel to ask how far they had gone.

"About ten miles," Rachel said. "Want a break?"

"Yes. You sure do cover a lot of ground."

They stopped at a sandy area with a few large rocks scattered around. Margaret came off her horse with a groan, knowing this would be a long-hot-bath night. She watched enviously as Rachel casually stepped off her horse to keep Margaret company. No groans there. Margaret looked at the horses and saw not a flared nostril nor patch of sweat. In this bunch, she was the identified wimp.

She had plopped herself down to the sand and started to stretch out her legs when she heard the rustle next to her. A tan and brown blotched snake, head reared, flicked its tongue at her. With a shriek, Margaret exploded out of the sand, scaring Fly Up into a snorting rear.

Rachel quickly came over to see what had frightened them.

Margaret said, "It's a rattlesnake. There in the grass." Unbelieving, she saw Rachel step into the cluster of grass and gently flip the snake out into the open, where it lay belly up. "You killed it. You didn't have to do that." Margaret looked angrily at Rachel.

Rachel couldn't stop herself from laughing, but she liked it that Margaret was angry. "It's a hognose snake. They play dead."

Margaret looked back at the snake regarding them with little agate slitted eyes. The snake turned itself over and slithered out of sight. "You knew all along, didn't you?" Margaret said, brushing some sand from her jeans and feeling a little embarrassed at her girlish shriek. She felt herself start to giggle and caught Rachel's eyes, and they were both laughing.

Margaret walked over to another rock and peered around it. Something scampered off, and she jumped. "All that slithers isn't snake," Rachel said.

"Very funny. This is quite a rest stop you've chosen."

"They are all as exciting as this one." Rachel took off her hat, smoothed her hair back, then replaced her Stetson, looking at Margaret from under the downturned brim. "Here, I'll come over and protect you." She sat down next to where Margaret was standing. Margaret sat warily next to her, and Rachel felt a warm glow come over herself that wasn't sun.

"Tell me about yourself," Margaret said, the boldness of the question she was about to ask making her short of breath. "Have you ever been with anyone?"

For a moment Rachel had an elk look about her. Will she bolt to the woods? Margaret thought.

"Well, I've never been married." Rachel fiddled with her rein ends, gazed out over the far vista, then flashed a look at Margaret. "What do you mean?" She quickly went on, "I've never shacked up with a guy. Never been that much of a fool. Love 'em and leave 'em," she laughed awkwardly. Margaret's direct look unnerved her.

"Is there anyone you have cared about romantically?" Margaret took her turn at fiddling, pushing her boot toe into the sand. "Maybe it's too personal a question."

Rachel struggled inside herself to stay sitting and answer. "Once is all. A long time ago, ancient history." Her laugh came out a little forced. "You gals from the East seem to go in for that romance stuff. When I want to get laid I just go to Lewiston and find me a lonely cowboy." It was too much for her. She stood up. "You rested long enough?"

"I guess so." Margaret smiled and held out a hand to be helped up. Rachel took it, feeling a hot electric energy meeting the dry surface of her palm and fingers. Margaret, standing before her, met her with the level blue eyes of a clear day. "I won't ask you any more personal questions if you don't want—"

"No, it's O.K."

"I would just like to know you better. I like you."

Rachel laughed shyly. "I guess I spend too much time just around horses. But for a human, you're all right." Damn, she thought, why do I feel like an awkward teenager? And then the answer came to her. *Because the last time I felt like this was with Amy.*

She tossed the far rein over Kestrel's neck and mounted up. Kestrel's familiar body between her legs reassured her. "Let's ride," Rachel said.

That night, feeling a nonspecific twinge of excitement as on the night before a competitive ride, Rachel put out the lights and went to bed. She lay there braiding and unbraiding the fringe on the wool blanket while she thought about Amy. It had been a long time since she had allowed herself to remember.

Amy's deft, competent hands were the first thing Rachel noticed about her. It was in art class their freshman year at Sweet Grass High School. Amy's family had moved from Maine to Montana, and Amy's vibrant watercolors of grass meeting mountains looked like the Atlantic Ocean meeting the rocky Maine coast.

Amy was an oddball from the start. She wore knee-high wool socks, obstinately out of step with the prescribed mid-calf white cotton bobby socks. Rachel soon joined the sock rebellion. Amy didn't curl or tease her hair. Never wore make-up. Out of school she always had on jeans and cowgirl boots. She didn't flirt with boys.

Rachel taught her to ride, and that spring and summer they

were inseparable. One rainy day they went to the barn loft, where, with the pigeons calling, their intimacy extended onto ground that left them both shaken with unfamiliar passion. A brief period passed filled with intense looks; hands trembling before touch; long, whispered telephone calls. Before either of them could absorb what had happened, Amy's parents quickly got out their pruning shears to nip this new love in the bud. Amy was sent to "visit an aunt" in Philadelphia and then enrolled in a boarding school in Vermont.

Rachel felt stunned by the loss of Amy. A yawning crevice opened up at her feet and ran through each day. For a few months she persistently wrote each day. Her letters never came back and were not answered.

Somehow, for Rachel, this experience was like a time capsule, forever separate from her "real" life. She knew that her experience with Amy was connected to her rising feelings for Margaret and that those feelings were bringing Margaret closer to her faster than she could take in. She felt confused.

Still, the warm deep place in her had been reached. It had been reopened like a cut healed only halfway to a scar.

Six

Saturday seemed like a normal day. Rachel's plan had been to sit on the porch, listen to her new Brahms concerto, and repair tack. Margaret was due to come out around noon to work Fly Up over some jumps on the lunge line. As the clock edged toward twelve o'clock, Rachel became increasingly nervous. Before she quite knew what she was doing, she found herself saddling Kestrel and riding out of the valley at a nice steady jog.

She pulled up at her favorite spy rock, surrounded by junipers —the scene of many unobserved stakeouts of the ranch when she was a kid. Lounging in the saddle, she crossed her right leg over the horn and leaned her elbow on it, chin on the knuckles. She sat there patiently waiting for Margaret's Toyota truck to pull into the barnyard.

"Why did I bolt?" she murmured to herself. "Kestrel, what am I doing here, do you know?" She knew she was afraid of what she was beginning to feel for Margaret, but every time she tried to grapple with it, her mind would skim off like a skipping stone to something else—like the hawk hanging and sliding through the air, now clear, now a speck. She watched it circle, then drop for prey. Straightening in the saddle, she turned the horse and rode on up the trail. "I know if I see her drive up, I'll want to go back down, and I need to sort out my wits," she told the spruce trees.

Rachel rode at a leisurely pace, remembering the young woman Amy, the innocence of it, her own overwhelming confusion afterward. Her experience with Amy had a tenderness about it, much different from her encounters with men. Margaret's gentle hand holding the new foal's foot suddenly filled her mind. Images past and present washed in and through her.

Her memory brook still running in her head, she dismounted at the real creek, gurgling through willows and cottonwoods, to let Kestrel drink. With one rein thrown over the mare's neck and the other draped over her shoulder, she ambled up the stream, stopping every once in awhile to gaze into the willow leaves or to push the moss off the rocks with her boot toe.

The rein slipped from her shoulder as Kestrel stopped, ears pricked. Then the horse gave a barrel-shaking whinney, loudly greeting a friend. An answering call came from just ahead in the trees. Through the trailing branches, Rachel could barely see Nanna hitched to a cart. A gasp drew her eyes to two entwined women in a bed of grass under a canopy of willow leaves, shimmering like a school of fishes.

Knowing their discovery was complete, Kate and Sarah sat up, their naked bodies flickering with freckled sunlight. One brown lean young body with watchful eyes under raven-black hair. One full startlingly pink body with frizzy curly brown hair. Sarah did the most comforting thing she could do for herself under the circumstances. She talked.

"Miss Duncan! How are you? We are having a really nice picnic. Would you care to join...umm? Are you having a lovely ride?" At that moment, Sarah could feel a gentle hand, small and cool on her thigh. The touch ended in a soft pat as she quieted.

Kate watched Rachel's back thread its way through the low-hanging branches. Small dunes of cottonwood fluff drifted in her wake. They heard the sound of hooves trotting steadily away.

Rachel rode back slowly in the general direction of the ranch. She had a lot to sort out for herself and was unskilled at naming her feelings. It was like reaching into a goldfish bowl. Just when she thought she had hold of one slippery fish, she realized there were more, and then they would swim into one of those dark little castles surrounded by algae.

She had known for some time that there was no intimacy in her sexual contacts with men. In fact, she had used them to blow off her sexual steam. She thought maybe her real intimacy had been with the girls who worked at the ranch. Not sexually, but nonetheless they were the ones she had learned the basics from. Some, like Kate, had taught her a lot.

She knew, now, that she was attracted to Margaret. Although she had been fighting off that knowledge for a while, feeling drawn to the woman was somehow easy; it was the complexity surrounding that one fact that was confusing. She would have expected herself to be shocked by seeing two women in a clearly sexual embrace, for example, but instead she found it comforting. Somewhere deep inside herself Rachel felt reassured.

Still, she fought off fitting in the final picture of the puzzle. Each piece was interesting, but that didn't have to mean that she was gay. It was probably a crush . . . like the one she had had for Amy. Rachel struggled, resisting the change that would come into her life if she allowed herself to fully embrace her feelings for Margaret.

She took a side trail to the west, then angled off the track to come out atop a ridge at her favorite view. The Crazy Woman Mountains, thirty miles or more to the south, always gave her some of their power.

Far off in the southwest, she could see a faint curl of smoke that must be coming from Jim's cooking fire. She studied it a minute to make sure. The fear of fire in this country was an ever-present one. The sun near overhead gave a flattened look to everything, as if a large iron had smoothed out the wrinkles. Soon, she knew, if she could stay quiet enough, the nearness of the horse would lend animal status to her, and all the other animals would go on about their lives.

Dismounting, she leaned against the comforting steadiness of the big creature, absorbing Kestrel's soft, unjudgmental presence. She sensed, then, that her ability to love, and her growing feelings for Margaret, deep and healthy, came from her animal place. They were simple things, part of life. It was self-hatred that was unnatural. She needed to be reminded— the loss of Amy had been cruel and painful, so wrong.

For the first time she saw the bleakness of her future with her random cowboys. "It sure ain't going to get any better with them," she said dryly. She flashed on Margaret reaching her hand out to her at their trail rest stop, and the dry, charged feeling of the touch.

Rachel's boot found the stirrup as she swung her leg over Kestrel's back. The horse dug her hooves into the rocky soil and took off at a gallop.

Rachel halted at the overlook to the ranch and counted the mare's breaths by the slight rocking of her body. She had pushed her a little too hard. Margaret's truck was not there. Either she hadn't come, or she was already gone. They started the slow switchbacks down to the valley floor, walking the last mile in. At the apricot trees Rachel dismounted and loosened Kestrel's cinch. The soft sweet scent of the blossoms swept with her as she led the mare by.

A loneliness crept in some time around the rubdown. "Why did I have to run off like that?" she asked Kestrel. She wondered when or if Margaret would be back.

The note she found on the kitchen table, pinned under a jar of chutney, said a lot: *How would you like me to make shrimp curry Friday at my place?* Rachel smelled the note for a trace of Margaret, then folded it small and tucked it in her shirt pocket.

Looking through her dog-eared, coffee-stained phone book, which was twelve years out of date because it would have been impossible to transfer all the notes to a new book, she finally found Margaret's number scribbled next to Dr. Stewart's old one.

"Answering for Dr. Carson." Rachel was speechless. "Hello? Is this an emergency?"

"No," Rachel croaked out, "I'll call back later." The confrontation of this stranger's voice when she had expected Margaret was more than she could handle.

Suddenly boots and jeans were too constricting for her. She peeled them off and put on a pair of shorts, going barefoot out into the warm spring sun. She stood for a moment in the tool shed attached to the garage, trying to decide what to do. Grandfather Duncan had drawn each tool's shape in black paint on the wall, mute reminders when some tool left for the great tool unknown. But most still hung there, waiting for a hand to reach for them and feel their oiled readiness to do the job. She took down the pruners and a small saw.

She clipped and sawed among the apple trees on the rise behind the house. The tiny green leaves framed the falling petals around her legs, white still from their winter hibernation. Soon the piles of branches weeded out from their sisters lay under the trees. Aunt Molly had said, "Prune out the center so a robin can fly through and not touch its wings."

The sound of Sarah's car engine starting brought Rachel back from her horticultural escape. She was not aware of having had any thoughts, just of the rhythm of the work. Standing back, she surveyed the apple trees she had just pruned, the branches reaching out with their tips angled down, the center open for sunlight and air and robins. Gathering up her tools and a few flowering branches, she walked down to the house.

Kate was waiting on the porch.

"Do you want me to go?" she asked, her eyes direct and proud.

Rachel's face was puzzled, concentrated, her head angled slightly forward. She was trying to figure out what Kate meant. Suddenly her mind cleared.

"Oh. Hell. You mean you and Sarah?" At a nod from Kate, Rachel barked out a laugh and shook her head. She reached over to give Kate a horse pat on the shoulder, grasped her arm, looked her in the eyes, and said, "You're O.K. with me, kid."

As the word *kid* came out of Rachel's mouth, she realized Kate was no longer one in her eyes. But it wasn't Kate who had grown, it was she. "I've got a lot to think about. Past few weeks have sort of shaken me out of my routine." Rachel's serious face gave way to a slow smile that changed all her angles into radiating creases from eyes and mouth.

Kate then understood that this conversation carried more than the discovery of Kate and Sarah's love for each other. Her whole body softened as she pushed herself away from the porch railing. To mark the end of the serious conversation, she had to make a joke.

"You better do something for those legs." Kate bent over to more closely examine the blue-veined paleness. "Looks like they died last week."

Rachel looked down with a grin. "Don't they."

Sunday night the rain started. It poured for two days and another night. The drenching rain made the outdoor chores shrink to the bare essentials; slogging around in a slicker and rubber boots wasn't much fun.

It was a good time to bring the new crop of four-year-olds into the barn for a refresher course. Each one was put on the crossties in the big center aisle, brushed, feet picked up, and the saddle lightly placed on its back with the cinch barely tightened.

"What do you think of this one?" Rachel asked Kate of a stocky bay mare standing fourteen hands.

Kate was delighted to have her opinion sought. "She might make a good distance horse for a kid." Kate ran her hands down the clean legs with beautiful bone, then stood back to look at the whole horse. The mare didn't have the long flat muscling of the long-distance runner. Hers was a more quarter-horse look with heavy, short muscle masses. "I think, though, that she might make a better reining or stock horse. Quick turns and stops might be her specialty. The old 'turn on a dime and give you back a nickel's change' horse."

Rachel smiled. "I think you've got a good eye. Let's turn her in with a few steers and see if she has any cow sense."

Finding out what "comes natural" to each horse was perhaps the biggest challenge for a trainer. The aim was to stay honest to the individuality of the horses, not to try forcing them into a track where they gave only a part of themselves, either physically or mentally.

Some people were naturals with words. Others felt lost, as if their mother tongue were a foreign language. Neither Kate nor Rachel was very strong in the verbal area. Both had, instead, a richly communicative nonverbal way that was part of their horse sense, part of what made them especially good trainers and horsewomen. During the few days of work inside the barn, their own sense of self and of the other shifted around. Kate found that she was watching Rachel's body for information on how Rachel really felt about Kate's lesbianism. Kate knew how much weight the words, *You're O.K. with me,* carried when every subtle signal was moving the speaker away. As Kate watched, Rachel told her in the language Kate trusted that she felt soft and open. If anything, she was more relaxed. Rachel's view of herself expanded, too. She understood what it was like to feel acceptance of another's difference and, with that, acceptance of the difference within herself.

Wednesday was, at best, not raining. After scraping the mud off Kestrel and Merlin, Kestrel's young nephew, they rode out, keeping to the high-crowned dirt roads leading to the town of Buffalo. One moment the wind out of the west would tease by with the scent of wild flowers and sage, only to be overcome the next by a fierce howling out of Canada with a sharp tundra snap. After an hour of walking and trotting, mixed with running beside the horses and using their big bodies to block the wind, Rachel said, "Had enough?"

A nod from Kate and they reined in unison toward the ranch, grateful the wind was mostly gnawing now at their backs. Collars up, hats pulled down, they hunched their bodies against the wind. It took a few moments for them to realize that what they were bracing themselves against had stopped. Heads turtling out and around, they saw patches of sunlight racing across the ground. On either side of the road, lakes had formed in the hollows. Nature was being playful again, forcing them to look at her changeability with new eyes. Soon the lakes would sink down into the grass roots, but now the occasional gusts of wind stirred their surfaces into oceans of whitecaps.

It took all of Rachel's adult restraint to ignore the siren call for a wild dash off the road. She looked over at Kate. A transparently child-devil grin passed between them. They bounded off the road, their shrieks and whoops echoing back to them off the ridges, a whole tribe of crazy women. The horses cow-hopped, wild-eyed, heads up, ears swiveling, landing hock-deep in the nearest puddle. Leaping up as the cold water hit their bellies, they bounded forward, sheets of water flying up on either side as if they were great sailing ships. Manes were sails; muzzles, bowsprits. Kate and Rachel rode as huntresses on the watch for the biggest puddle.

"There, over there, look." Kate's pointing hand was enough

for Merlin. From a snorting stand to a full tearing gallop, he made for the white-capped ocean. All worry left the women's bodies, and they flew like seabirds. Their bird shrieks soared on toward other oceans as they slowed to a walk and became Amazon horsewomen again. The horses, still wired, saw sharks in plain grey rocks and hurtling sea monsters in rolling tumbleweed.

Breathless and warmed, the two women rode side by side at a walk, trying to bring the horses back to old familiar Montana. They rode along, relaxed and talking comfortably, until Kate mentioned that Sarah was coming over Friday. A soft deep groan came from Rachel.

Kate immediately bridled. "Hey. I thought you didn't have any problem with Sarah being here." She looked sharply at Rachel, who had sunk into her sheepskin coat.

"No," came from the coat. "I've got a stomachache."

"There is some flu going around."

"Maybe that's it. Last couple of days it's been on and off. Haven't had much of an appetite. Everything tastes like cardboard. Whenever I think of that shrimp dinner Margaret's invited me to on Friday, I think I'm going to throw up."

Since Kate had witnessed Rachel eat, that very morning, three fried eggs, half a mounded plate of home fries, and six pieces of bacon, washed down by a pint of orange juice and three cups of coffee, she wasn't too worried. She thought the problem might have more to do with Margaret than with the shrimp.

"Well, look," Kate said, "how about I fix us dinner tonight? We could play a game of Trivial Pursuit, or chess."

Rachel smiled at her. "I'd like that. What's for dinner?"

"I just found this terrific recipe for chicken mole. It's a Peruvian Indian dish—you'll know you're not eating cardboard." Kate grinned devilishly as she jumped off Merlin and wrapped the reins over the hitching rail.

Seven

Shrimp Dinner Day dawned. Rachel felt scattered through-out it, starting some small simple job, then wandering off to half-finish another project. The hours melted away, dragging and disjointed. She came to around four o'clock, realizing she had forgotten to ride Kestrel. There wasn't time now. She went to find Kate.

"Look, Kate, you know I've got this dinner with Margaret to-night in Judith Gap."

How could I forget? Kate thought as she nodded. *She's been a basket case all day.*

"Kestrel needs a spin-out. Ten miles or so ought to do it. I didn't get to it today."

Small wonder. Kate nodded helpfully.

"Do you mind doing it for me?"

"No problem," Kate said, thinking it was probably a good thing. In the state Rachel was in, she could ride over the hill and be lost some place around Glacier National Park.

"Thanks."

"Have fun tonight. Sarah is coming over later, so I'll get Kestrel up now."

"Bye," Rachel said, slightly glazed and distracted. She went into the house to shower and change. By the time she was dressed, rejected clothes lay all over the bed, flung off after one look in the mirror. She finally ended up, mostly out of exasper-ation, with a two-tone blue satin rodeo shirt with pearl buttons and clean jeans of a recent vintage, the leather belt clasped by an award buckle from the Big Horn ride. She found socks without holes and stomped into her city boots, irritated with herself for taking so long in her private fashion show.

Looking in the full-length mirror, a flash of memory came to her, sharp and painful. She was standing here dressed for the junior high school Roundup Days Dance, her father behind her. He had come into the room to tell her that Jim Boyce and his mom were there to pick her up. Rachel had said, "How do I look, Dad?"

He had replied, "Like a cat that's been out in the rain. Why don't you curl your hair? And that dress is too short." Whenever she sat down that night she had tugged at the hem.

Rachel stalked to the truck with a fierce face, hoping to forestall any teasing from Kate. She was feeling very silly and keyed-up. Fortunately, Kate wasn't around to see her carefully dust off the seat before she climbed in. Then she bombed out the road, late from all her primping.

Sarah, arriving early, pulled off the road when she saw the truck with a rooster-tail plume careening toward her. Rachel passed her at the cattle guard with a crisp salute of a wave, her face still fierce.

Sarah watched in the rearview mirror as the truck disappeared, trailing a cloud of dust that enveloped and filtered into her Datsun like a beige fog.

"She's mad. She doesn't want me to come here." Stunned, Sarah rapidly tried to think how this would affect Kate and their time together. She knew how much Kate liked her employer. In the phone call after they were discovered, Kate had said Rachel was fine about "it." But now Sarah thought Kate must have gotten it wrong.

She drove on down the road with great foreboding. When she got out of her little orange car, she did her best to shake off the fine dust. Turning the side mirror, she tried to see how she looked, but it gave back a carnival distortion. She read the small print at the bottom of the mirror: *Objects appear closer than they are.* She shook her head. "Ain't it the truth. You think you know what's happening, then whammo. You find out it's not what you thought at all."

Kate wasn't in the bunkhouse. "I bet she's in the barn sur-

rounded by those thousand-pound monsters she loves so much."
Sarah cautiously opened the barn door as if a hundred horses
would burst out and trample over her prone body. It was quiet
and dark inside. She called out a thin little "Hello?"

"Sarah. You're early. Come on in." Kate laughed with sym-
pathetic humor. "There is just Kestrel on the cross-ties. You can
sit here on this hay bale."

Sarah crept in, stood ten feet away from the horse, the hay
bale being much too near, and said, "Will she kick me?"

Kate pounced on her, wrapping her arms around Sarah, gave
her a kiss, and said, "She won't kick you. I'm the one who's dangerous to be around." She nibbled Sarah's neck where the curly
fuzz met an earlobe, then proceeded to lick and whuffle her way
over the shoulder down to the deep line of Sarah's blouse, where
the triangle of shadow drew her like a bat to a cave. She felt the
rumble of laughter under her lips, and tilted her head back to
see what was amusing the object of her attentions.

"Oh, I don't think I'm in danger around you." Sarah slid her
fingers through Kate's hair.

Kate's eyebrows flicked up. "Oh no? Well then, come see the
new baby." She led Sarah by the hand to Sparrow Hawk's stall.

Sarah stood by the stall door, trying to translate the mare's
body language. "Will she be mad if I look at her baby?"

"Oh no. She loves showing off her daughter. Come on in the
stall."

Sarah sidled in and was delighted when Dawn came up to
her and sniffed her with a whiskery little nose. "Will she bite?"

"She doesn't have much in the teeth department yet. Besides,
horses are vegetarians, like you, and don't go around casually
chomping on people. They only bite when they are angry. Un-
like me," Kate added.

Kate lightly brushed off the mare, then sprayed her with insect repellent. "The mosquitoes have been ferocious since the
rain."

"That reminds me, Rachel looked positively deadly when I
saw her on the road. I thought she didn't mind if I came out here."

"Hey, that didn't have anything to do with you. She is a mess
because she's having dinner tonight with that gorgeous new

veterinarian."

Relief followed by a little pout of jealousy came over Sarah's face. "How gorgeous?"

Kate touched her gently on the arm, her brown hand silhouetted on Sarah's white Mexican blouse. "To me, there is no one in the world more beautiful than you."

They were interrupted by barking from Woody, for once noticing that a car had arrived at the ranch. Kate set the insect repellent bottle down with the brush on the grooming shelf next to Kestrel. "I'll go see what they want."

A family of five poured out of the four-door sedan. "We are looking for a horse for our daughter and heard Miss Duncan might have one for sale. Are you she?" the man asked.

"No. She's away right now." Kate tried to find out what level of riding the child had managed to attain, but it was uphill work to make a realistic assessment.

"Mary Beth can ride anything," the mother said. "She has won ribbons in shows."

"How nice for her," Kate said, casting a quick glance at the smug subteen draped against the side of the car.

The father pointed at the paddock where the yearlings were lounging about after their evening feed. "That brown one looks like a nice pony."

Kate's eyes mentally rolled. It took her fifteen minutes to finally get rid of these horse consumers, advising them to call the following day.

Sarah listened to the strained conversation and grew restless with waiting. As she sat amid the beasts that had so frightened her, she decided it was time to overcome her fear. She felt at a disadvantage in this overwhelmingly horsey world. She took up the brush and tentatively stroked it over Kestrel's hide. Made bold by the horse's quiet acceptance, she picked up the spray bottle and misted the repellent everywhere it felt safe to reach. She was proud of herself when Kate came back and found her spraying the legs.

"Maybe we'll make a horsewoman of you yet," Kate teased. When she had the mare saddled, she asked, "Do you mind starting dinner while I'm gone? This will take me a little over an hour.

There's some tofu in the fridge and vegetables in the crisper."
Sarah nodded, feeling competent and ranch-wifely.

Rachel moved the headless shrimp into the rice on her plate.
She reached for the chutney jar, spooning out more of the pungent fruit, trying to hide the accusing shellfish.
"Do you like it?"
"Mostly. It's real different. Where did you get this chutney?
I never had anything like it."
"I made it when I was on vacation in Vermont," Margaret answered. "A. . .umm. . . friend and I rented a cabin for a couple of weeks. There was a huge overflowing garden next to it. The owners said we could take anything we wanted. Leeks, tomatoes, jalapeño peppers galore. So we bought some cider vinegar, ginger, brown sugar, and raisins, and chopped and boiled and filled jars for a week." Margaret's face changed from the moment of the memory to a sad, guarded look.
Rachel studied her. More to this story, she thought.
"Well, it's good. Real tasty." Rachel took the plunge, speared the shrimp covered with chutney, and got it down. "So what brought you out here?"
"I wanted a change. A totally new place." And to get away from Trudy and all the things that reminded me of her, Margaret thought but couldn't say.
"You got that, I expect. Must have been hard, though, to leave friends and family. You had family out east?"
"Yes, my father is a gynecologist in Boston. Mother's only interest seems to be the social gambit. I much preferred working with my father on his racing cars." Margaret gave a funny lopsided grin. "Not my mother's choice. She hounded me to get married. So that's part of why I came out to these wilds."
"What's the other part?" Rachel asked with startling boldness.
Margaret gave her a long look, trying to decide how much to tell her. "A painfully failed relationship." She got up immediately to clear the table. "Would you like coffee?"
Rachel could recognize a boundary when she saw one.
"Sounds great." She settled deeper into her chair. "Well, you know I had a close call, too." She tried to tell from Margaret's back if

she was interested. A noise came from that general direction which sounded vaguely like encouragement. "I met this guy Steve on the rides. He lives up Missoula way. Had a wife that ran off to California, took me awhile to see why. He got it into his head that I was his next woman. I was flattered enough that I got kind of interested. He had some nice horses. We hung around together, but pretty soon I found the only thing we had in common was the horses. He couldn't put one sentence together. Talked in grunts. He expected me to do for him. You know, shirt buttons and such. Hell, I told him, I barely had time to sew on my own. But I guess what finished me was I was bored and it was a struggle just to keep him down to an occasional toss in the sheets. I finally figured it was more trouble than it was worth."

Rachel looked up and was surprised to see Margaret leaning against the sink, her Greek blade of a nose slicing down between her eyes, her lips just softly curving in a smile. "Mine was a woman." Margaret said clearly.

"What?"

"A woman. My close call was named Trudy." She paused to give Rachel time to take it in. Maybe to give myself time, too, she thought.

Rachel gathered herself and tried to look innocent. "Oh, yeah? Gay? I never knew anyone. . . ." Honesty got the better of her. "Until recently." She ground to a stop. She tried hard not to show how pleased she was with this information and ended up by blushing and rearranging her boots.

Margaret poured the boiling water over the ground coffee beans and thought, Oh shit, I've blown it. She's going to tell every goddamned rancher in the state that I'm a dyke. She set up the empty cups on their matching saucers, gifts her mother had intended for Margaret's bridal chest. In the thick silence it was clear when the last drop of water had seeped through the coffee filter. Margaret poured out the coffee and set a cup and saucer of the thinnest bone china, painted with doves and flowers, in front of Rachel.

Rachel wanted to touch Margaret and tell her that she understood, in fact welcomed this information. Instead, she reached over to pet El Gordo, sitting on the chair beside hers. The cat slid out from under her hand when the telephone rang. "It's for you," Margaret said, holding out the receiver. Rachel stood with alarm. The only person who knew where she was tonight was Kate. "Must be trouble," she muttered.

She listened tensely as Kate told of coming back from her ride, Kestrel's back seeming to be sore after she took off the saddle, giving the mare a liniment rubdown only to find that almost immediately big blisters appeared on her back. "By God, I don't know what the problem is. Just a minute." Rachel related all this to Margaret.

Margaret took the phone. "Almost sounds like a chemical burn. Put ice in a pillowcase and lay it over a wet towel on her back. Keep it on until we get there. I want to see this."

Margaret hung up the phone, then went into the bathroom to get her aloe vera hand lotion. "You are going to miss dessert," she said, as she put on her shoes.

"I don't mind."

"It's fabulous rhubarb upside-down cake I slaved over for you."

"Bring it."

They both laughed for a minute at themselves.

"Look, I'm going on ahead," Rachel said.

"I'm hot on your tail," Margaret double-entendred.

Margaret, her hands tenderly palpating the blisters, kept shaking her head. "What the hell caused this?" she asked. Rachel and Kate both shook their heads. Rachel said, "I've never seen anything like it." Kestrel's back sank painfully at the lightest touch. Large blisters filled with fluid covered her back. Sarah stood unnoticed off to one side, her evening ruined, the stir-fry now mush.

"It looks like a chemical burn, a reaction to something. What did you wash the saddle blankets in? Anything new? A detergent not rinsed out enough could cause this."

"They are washed in a mild wool soap. Nothing has changed about that." Rachel's mind raced over any change in the routine that could have caused these burns.

Margaret dropped her arms to her side. "All right, let's go over every little thing that happened tonight. The smallest detail could be important. What brushes did you use, for instance?"

Kate turned to the shelf. "This one. Doesn't look like it has anything on it." She smelled it.

"Then what happened?" Margaret prodded.

"Some people came to see the horses. I told them to come back tomorrow when you were here." She turned to Rachel, the agony on her face showing her sense of responsibility.

"Did they come in the barn?"

"No. When I came back, I put the saddle on, then rode out."

Margaret put her hands over her eyes and breathed deeply. "What could have caused this?" she desperately asked.

A very small voice asked, "Do you think it was because I sprayed her with fly repellent?"

Three sets of eyes bored into Sarah. "You did? On her back?" came from all three women simultaneously. Sarah started to cry.

"That's it," Margaret said, going to her truck for the hand lotion she had brought on a hunch.

"Damn," Rachel said, thinking of the weeks it would take before she could once again put a saddle on the mare's back. She would have to "pony" her, lead her from another horse's back, to keep her fit. "Damnation," she said again.

Sarah's crying mounted to a wail. "I'm so sorry, Miss Duncan. I didn't mean to hurt your horse."

"I know that."

"I saw Kate spray it on the mother horse and thought it would help her out. Oh dear, I felt so brave and now I've ruined everything."

Kate did her best to soothe Sarah but was not very effective. Margaret came back with a shiny stainless steel bucket.

"I need this full of lukewarm water." She held it out to Kate.

Sarah grabbed it. "Let me please," she said, and ran off to the house.

Margaret outlined what she was going to do to treat the problem. "First, I'm going to wash off all traces of the fly spray and liniment with a mild soap. Then when her back is dry, I'll cover the area with this aloe-based hand cream. You will need to get some more of this and keep smearing it on until there is no more sensitivity." She explained that using baby oil would keep the heat in, aggravate it. "This may take as long as two weeks to heal."

Rachel thought about the Bitterroot ride three weeks away. She stared at the mare's back as Margaret poured the soapy water, a cup at a time, slowly, gently, not actually touching her back. The creamy rivulets ran down the hair grain to the whorls to drain off in little waterfalls. "Let's take her outside to rinse her off with the hose."

By the time Kestrel's back was dry, and lotion gobbed thickly over it, night had fallen. "Keep her out of the sun during the hot part of the day," Margaret instructed, putting away her gear.

"Do you think she might be able to do a ride in three weeks?"

"I don't know. The next three days or so will tell a lot."

The four women stood around, their respective evenings turning out much differently than anticipated. A let-down, hole-in-the-day feeling left them not knowing what to do next. Margaret reached to the seat of her truck to bring out a towel-covered pan.

"So who wants dessert?"

Rachel sighed, glad Margaret wasn't just running off. "Come on up to the house, everybody. I'll make some coffee."

A sober group filed into the kitchen, Kate still trying to comfort Sarah, Margaret and Rachel wary from their interrupted conversation. As social occasions went, the only thing that was successful was the cake.

Rachel finally said, "Why don't you two go on off to the bunkhouse? I know you want to be alone." She, of course, also wanted to be alone with Margaret.

Margaret looked at her sharply. *Rachel knows about them,* she thought. *Maybe I've read her wrong.*

When the younger women had left, Rachel picked up the thick white coffee cups and said, "Let's go into the living room." She sat on the sofa and left the big chair for Margaret. "You know, I've been on a treadmill a lot of my life. Lately, it's been different. What you talked about—Trudy—well, I'd like to know more. I've just learned that Kate and Sarah are gay."

"Gay is mostly the term used for men who love each other.

We usually call ourselves lesbian."

"Lesbian. You know, I've always wondered why. . . I mean, there are so many terms people use." Rachel tapered off to silence. Margaret smiled warmly, "Then I'll tell you. There once was a poet, Sappho, who lived on the island of Lesbos. She wrote beautiful love poems to women, and the women living there were called Lesbians."

"This really happened?" Rachel was dumbfounded.

"Yes, it really did. At the height of ancient Greek culture. But it is happening now. There are women today writing love poems to women all over the world. There is a lot more acceptance and openness in the last ten years. I don't know why I told you. I guess I thought I could. . . or needed you to know. It's very hard sometimes keeping such an important part of yourself under-cover."

Rachel looked at her, openly and with humor. "So don't keep yourself under wraps. Sometimes it challenges me out of my narrow little world, but I like you so I want to know. Tell me about Trudy." She saw the memory of pain come into Margaret's face. "But only if you want to."

"Failed relationships are always sad stories." Margaret took a deep breath. "It slowly fades. Trudy and I loved each other at the start. And we both loved horses. Although we had our differences even there, it was also where we came together. She was afraid of being close and yet wanted it so much, it was push and pull the whole time. And she would have affairs—I think to convince herself that she really was separate. It worked. I felt more and more separate. Each one took a piece of me. It hurt so much, but I wanted to leave before I hated her. I had been working in a practice with two other vets in Saratoga. Once I had my vet school bills paid and enough money saved to buy into a private practice, there was nothing keeping me there. I had to put some miles between us." She looked at Rachel and found her riveted to every word. "I still love Trudy, but the physical distance helps. It just wasn't working for me—I know the release from that relationship was the right thing."

"That must be hard, to love someone and not be able to be with them. . . her."

"It gets easier. I feel sad often, but as time passes I wonder if the love I thought I felt for her was really my own vulnerability. She was the first woman I was truly open to." Margaret paused. "Being that open made it difficult to protect myself from getting hurt. She became involved with one of my friends, and they both disappeared behind a wall of silence. I felt raw and bleeding, and I knew she was feeling no pain or loss." Margaret stood and ran her hand along the edge of the mantelpiece. "I think sometimes the loss of respect and real affection is harder than the loss of the actual person. There are also times you just have to get on with your life. This is one of them."

"It's late and you must be tired. If you want to stay here, there is a spare room," Rachel was careful to point out.

"Thanks, but I think I'll push off home. And thanks for listening to me. I hope you didn't get more than you bargained for. I sort of went on, didn't I?"

"Not at all. It was a hectic evening. Kestrel aside, I enjoyed it."

"Keep in touch with me about how she is recovering." Margaret reached out shyly to take Rachel's hand.

"Yes, I'll do that." Holding Margaret's hand, Rachel found herself reluctant to let go the realness of the contact. The moment her mind became aware of this, her hand opened suddenly to release Margaret without waiting for that subtle, mutually agreed upon signal that says it's time. She moved to the door and said, "Thanks for coming over. Good night."

"Good night."

Margaret went through the circle of light from the porch into the dark to her truck. Driving out the long driveway, she let the impression of the whole evening imprint itself on her. A night hawk skittered up in front of her when the lights hit it, and Margaret thought how like Rachel it was. *She has been private for so long. She has a lot of courage, though, to talk with me about what is so strange to her. I like her. Oh, come on, you know it's more than like.*

She squirted the windshield washer, then ran the wipers for a minute to clear the dust and to give herself something to do. *Does that make it any clearer?* She laughed at herself. *Maybe this is just that old rebound from Trudy. A need to clear her out of my attic.*

But Margaret didn't really think so. There was more to this rancher affair, and she knew it.

Rachel, her hands in soapy water, stood transfixed by the image looking back at her from the darkened mirror of the window. Speaking out loud to herself, she watched the fuzzy lips move with a detached interest. "It's probably because she reminds me of my mother. Amy was from the East, too." That reticence, that reserve. The kind of formal, graceful way she moved her body. The New England upper-class accent that almost sounded British to Rachel's ear. "Could that be why I am so drawn to her? That I'm trying to regain my mother?"

She let the water out of the sink, the suck of the last bit leaving the suds behind. She ran the faucet full-blast, rinsing out the sink. Then she dried her hands on the dishtowel.

A slow grin crept over Rachel's face. "Bullshit," she said and went to bed.

Eight

Fortunately, the moon was full over the next week. Rachel ponied Kestrel at night, leading her from Storm Queen, then turning her out to graze. During the day she was confined to a stall to keep her out of the sun and away from the bugs, who must have thought she smelled delicious. The blisters were down by the end of the week, her back still sensitive but improving every day. At the end of two weeks there was no sign of tenderness, so Rachel tried her light competitive saddle on a six-mile ride. No problems. She would keep her entry in the Bitterroot ride.

The only hitch was a call from Betty Dorset to say that she would be unable to caretake the ranch that weekend. Kate had to stay. It would mean scratching Grey Crow from the ride, planned as his first competition exposing him to the air crackling with super-fit horses and riders pitched to win. Often the stress of excitement took a greater toll than the miles. His shakedown cruise would have to wait. Rachel would go alone with Kestrel.

She found Kate in the small corral, riding one of the four-year-olds. Rachel watched as Kate gently encouraged the young horse to walk in circles both ways and to stand quietly. "No muss, no fuss," Rachel said softly, with a grin. She never could figure out why so many trainers expected a bucking-bronco scene the first time on a horse. Give it enough room to understand what you want, and they rarely fall apart. It was panic that made them buck.

Rachel waited until Kate dismounted, then walked up to help

take off the tack. They both gave the grey colt a lot of attention, scratching him in the most satisfying places until his lips quivered with pleasure. They stood by the gate as he galloped off to rejoin his buddies.

"I don't tell you often enough, Kate, how much I like the way you handle the horses. You have a kind, calm touch they respond to."

Kate smiled with pleasure. "I sure have a fine teacher. I hadn't seen anyone handle horses the way you do until I came here. Most people set it up like a battle of wills. Your horses want to give you everything they can."

"Our mutual appreciation society." They both laughed. "Actually, I came down here with some bad news. I just found out that Betty can't be here for the Bitterroot ride."

Kate's face registered disappointment.

"There is a twenty-five-mile ride in the Gallatin National Forest coming up pretty soon, though. It would be a way to introduce Grey Crow to competition. I could stay here and maybe Sarah could go with you. As a matter of fact, if she wants to stay here this coming weekend, it's fine with me. What do you think?"

"That sounds great, really. It's the Big Horn ride in two weeks I especially want to do."

"O.K. Why don't you call the ride manager and see if you can get an entry to Gallatin? I better hitch up the trailer and take it into the garage today. Maybe Mike can fit it in."

Rachel managed with only two tries to back up the truck so that the ball of the hitch lined up with the bulldog receiver on the trailer. Letting the jack down to engage the hitch, she idly wondered how many times she had done this. *Beyond counting.* The lights plugged in, she kicked the chucks out from between the tires.

Ninety minutes later the bell rang as the door to the garage opened. "Hey, Mike, are you in there?"

"Over here," Mike said, rolling out from under a green truck.

"Trailer needs some work. Have any time today to put on a new tire and fix a light?"

"Yeah, I can get to it in about an hour. You got some errands to run?"

Laughing, she said, "You bet I do."

"Soon as I finish the doc's truck, I'll start on yours."

She took another look at the truck. "Dr. Carson's?"

"Yeah. Boy, is she hard on the suspension. You have her out to your place yet?"

"She came a couple of times. Did a good job with a rough foaling."

"People seem to like her. 'Course, there are those who won't call her on account of her being a woman. They don't figure she has the strength to do the job." Mike unabashedly reported this to Rachel, seemingly unaware that he accepted her simply as one of the ranchers.

"She's plenty strong enough. Besides, it's brains that count." Rachel felt herself flush with righteous anger and then, with honesty, reminded herself of her earlier position. "Well, people who feel that way are missing out. I better start on those errands. See you later, Mike."

"Wait, umm. . .you know the wife's visitin' her mother in Helena. Think you might like to, you know, maybe get together tonight?"

Rachel's eyes skimmed the small garage as she said in a tight voice, "No, Mike, I don't think I will." Struggling for something to bring the normal banter back, she said, "Thought you were going to get rid of that calendar with the skimpy-dressed gal selling chainsaws."

He grunted as he slid back under Margaret's Toyota.

Rachel, sitting on a concrete bench in the little park by the library, felt intense embarrassment from the reminder of her nights with Mike. And the others. The times she would drive on auto pilot to a bar, get drunk, and get laid. She flushed remembering the fumbling scrambles to get them to put a condom on. The groping quick bursts of hot-breathed contact in the backs of cars, or the sharp stubble of hay fields in her back. Secretive. Like teenagers with no place to go for privacy. Always before the actual encounter she would feel her own strong lust. It didn't matter who it was, it nearly always went unsatisfied, except by herself.

The list in her hand stared up at her, mundanely sterile. Library. Groceries. All else neatly lined through. She would buy the groceries at the mall on the way out of town. The library lay ahead. She savored her monthly trips in through the heavy oak doors to the quiet, marble-lined, vaulted room. Built in the early 1900s by Croatian stonemasons, and paid for by Mr. Carnegie, it was a booklover's retreat. The mosaic-colored books waited, holding their riches for her.

She felt annoyed when she realized someone was sitting down next to her. The annoyance dissolved into total pleasure when she saw it was Margaret. They both said "Hi" at the same moment.

"How's Kestrel? Are you going to make your ride?"

"She's fine. I've been using my light saddle on her this whole week. Thanks."

A hiatus descended. *What to talk about now?* Rachel started gathering up her books. Margaret wasn't quite ready for her to leave. Awkwardly, she asked, "Oh, what are you reading?"

Rachel shifted her books to try to hide the titles. She was always a little embarrassed that she liked mysteries. "Just some novels. . .the new Dick Francis."

"Oh, let's see. It's one I haven't read. Are you taking it out or back?"

"I'm done with it."

"Great. I was wanting a good book to take with me to a conference I'm going to in Missoula. It will get me through those awful evenings when everyone 'socializes.' "

"When is it?"

"This coming weekend. I think I have a ride there with John McCoy."

"That letch. Look, the ride I'm doing is in the Bitterroots, just south of Missoula. Kate's got to stay at the ranch. Want to ride down with me?" Rachel found herself asking. To her amazement, Margaret looked delighted.

"Yes, that would be fun. I would like to see one of these rides up close."

They made the drive in a little over four hours, slow because of the horse trailer, but not minding. There was a lot they wanted to know about each other. When they drove through the Butte area, Margaret was shocked at this devastated part of Montana. She raged at the raw, unhealed rape that mining had left behind. The memory of it haunted her as they pulled into the Elkhorn Ranch, framed to the west by the glorious Bitterroots, showing the contrast of generations of loving stewardship of the land.

Rachel found a place to park on the far side of the grounds, shaded with towering old cottonwoods. The first thing she did was set up the portable electric fence with Margaret's help. They could hear an occasional restless stamp from the trailer as they worked. Rachel rigged the battery to the fence charger, then dropped the ramp and backed Kestrel out. The mare walked the boundary of the fence and then sent a ringing challenge of a neigh to the other horses she could see.

"Looks like she knows what she's here for," Margaret said.

"That she does," Rachel replied, moving to unhitch the trailer. "She gets as keyed up as I do before a ride."

She started unloading her gear and bedroll from the truck. Margaret came over and began taking out her bags.

"Aren't you going to need to keep your stuff in the truck?"

"I thought I'd rather come back here for the night. I hate staying in motels. Unless I'd be in the way?"

"Well, it's pretty rough. I just sleep in the horse trailer."

"That's fine with me. I don't have to be at the conference until nine tomorrow. I'd like to help around here and watch the vetting."

"O.K. If you don't mind shoveling out manure from the trailer, it'll have time to air out before we make our beds."

"I've shoveled manure before," Margaret answered with a grin.

"Good. I'll go get some water." Rachel set off with two large plastic buckets.

It seemed like a long time later that she came back, water sloshing over the brims. "I don't know why the water is always at the exact opposite of the grounds from where I park. But it's not crowded here either." She set one bucket out in the sun and put the other under the fence for Kestrel. Opening the front escape door to get some hay, she saw that Margaret had removed the center partition and tied it to one wall.

"More friendly this way," Margaret said. "It looked like a giant bundling board."

It came to Rachel, seeing the bedrolls ready to spread out side by side, that they would be very close. She gulped. "Looks cozy," she managed to say, then ducked back out and threw some hay to Kestrel. "I'm going to sign in and get my number."

"Hold on. I want to come too."

They found the ride management under a green-and-white tent set up near the creek. Rachel showed Kestrel's health papers, got her ride packet—rules, map, and numbered pennie—and found that vetting was going in order of sign-up. Four horses were ahead of her.

Margaret returned with her to help get Kestrel ready. Sliding a halter on the mare, Rachel asked Margaret to dig out the grooming kit. Using water from the bucket she had placed in the sun, she sponged off the manure stains from Kestrel's hocks, then picked out and washed her feet. Her mane and tail needed more brushing after the ride in the trailer. People complained about white horses being hard to keep clean, but Rachel didn't mind. They were so beautiful, it made up for the work.

Rachel changed her shirt and tied on her number twenty-eight pennie. "How do we look?" she asked.

"If the pair of you could win on looks alone, you'd have it hands down."

"We won't look this good at the end of the ride, I guarantee you." They grinned at each other.

Margaret watched as Rachel stood Kestrel for the two judges. One did legs; the other, body. They felt and examined every square inch of the horse, calling out to their respective recorders anything they found. "Tendons, clean, cold, tight." "Small bug bite right girth area." An eyelid was lifted: "Zero mucous membranes." The skin on the neck pinched: "Zero dehydration."

"Please trot her out for us straight away, straight back, then a figure eight," one of the judges asked. Height and length of stride, tail carriage, everything that could be written about the way she moved was recorded to be compared with how she looked after fifty miles.

Margaret was impressed. She stayed to watch more horses go through. In a lull between horses she introduced herself and found that one of the judges was a veterinarian, the other a "lay" judge: an experienced rider, this year recovering from a broken ankle, she was judging instead of competing.

They were both very friendly and explained the judging sheets to Margaret. The scorecard was divided into three boxes: one for body; one for legs; the third for way of going, or lameness. All of the original notes would be compared at the final vetting, with any change marked off the starting score of one hundred. Twenty minutes after crossing the finish line the pulse and respirations, known as P&Rs, were counted and figured against a baseline parameter set by the judges for the terrain and weather conditions. The horse was then vetted out in order of finish.

Dehydration was evaluated by pinching the skin on neck or shoulder, then counting how long it took to snap back to smooth. Zero was excellent; a count to three, life-threatening. Most horses came back with a one count on hot days. Margaret began to understand the importance of the water stops. She was fascinated by the thoroughness and clarity of this sport. She watched as eyelids were lifted for the mucous-membrane check, again zero to three on redness. Capillary-refill ability was checked by lifting the horse's upper lip, pressing the thumb to the gums, and seeing how long they took to return to pink. Each horse was judged only against itself.

A man came up leading a sorrel quarter horse with bulging muscles. The gelding put his ears back when the judges approached. The man jiggled the halter, but the horse wasn't reassured. As the judge reached to feel its legs, the beast cow-kicked at her. It took a while to go over the animal, but with patience it was finally managed.

"This your first ride? A rookie?"

"Yeah."

"Well remember, to finish is to win," Joyce, the legs judge, said.

"Oh, Ace will show these skinny-legged Arabs what a real Western horse can do. I ride him all the time."

"Good luck," Betty responded. After the pair had left, she commented to Margaret, "He will do well to bring that horse in sound in ride time."

"Hey, you ready for some dinner?" Rachel asked, coming up behind Margaret.

"Now that you mention it, I'm famished."

"There's a pretty good Chinese restaurant about ten minutes away. You like Szechwan?"

"Sounds great," Margaret replied.

Over dinner Margaret talked about how interesting it was for her. "I would be willing to bet I'll learn as much here as I do at the conference."

"Maybe. This is a warm-up for the Tevis in this area. Some good horses are here today."

They talked until Rachel noticed it was eight o'clock and said she needed to turn in. Her morning started at four with feeding Kestrel.

They were both a little self-conscious undressing for bed that night. Rachel put on a pair of her father's blue-and-maroon-striped pajamas. She was slightly shocked to see that Margaret slept nude. She tried not to watch as Margaret shucked off her jeans and T-shirt, busying herself setting her portable alarm. The moon came quietly in the side windows. Kestrel munched her hay at their feet in the steady calming way of horses. The sweet smell of hay and the rich warm pungent odor of fresh manure wafted into their odd bedroom. Lying there tucked in beside each other, they smiled—easy, relaxed. Margaret sat up, leaned over, and kissed Rachel on the forehead. "Good night," she said.

Rachel went to sleep glowing with warmth.

It took a few jangled minutes to find the travel clock and turn it off. The moon had long since traveled on, leaving a chilly predawn darkness. Reaching behind her, Rachel grabbed the bucket with grain measured out the night before. Rising, she picked up three flakes of hay and went barefoot down the ramp to set them down for Kestrel. She slid her hand down the inside edge of the water bucket and found that the mare had drunk well. Rachel snuggled back into her bag, her cold, dew-damp feet grateful for the warmth still there, and lay back, listening to the horse again settle in to her feed.

Margaret had fallen back to sleep. Rachel tried to, but her mind wasn't willing. She could hear the rumble of a rig arriving in time to ready the horses before the last horses were vetted through. That would start at 6:00. Preride briefing, when the last horse was done, probably around 7:00. Leave around 7:30. First horse back about 4:30. Two hours for vetting out would make the awards banquet about 6:30 or 7:00. Long day. She had to remember to eat the hard-boiled egg, granola bar, and banana that were in the cooler.

A van pulled in with the sound of a large expensive cat. Rachel could just see the running lights as it crept by. Dwight Newton's rig, she thought, a traveling palace carrying three horses on the diagonal, with rooms for tack and feed. She had been in it once, invited to celebrate his victory in the Green Mountain hundred-mile ride. Curiosity had temporarily overcome her distaste for the man, arrogant and condescending to the other riders and to the "working students" who rode his backup horses. *Palace* was not an exaggeration compared with the way most people bivouacked. The van had its own water tank, hot shower, and microwave oven along with the rest of the kitchen. There was a living room into which four comfortable beds could be let down from the wall. And, of course, an electric generator to support it all.

Which was humming now.

Margaret stirred. "What's that?" she asked.

"Dwight Newton," Rachel said, not too informingly.

"Oh. Well, do you think there is any coffee?"

"I could use a cup myself. I'll go look."

She pulled on her rubber boots and a sweater. Tracking across the damp grass in the unfocused early dawn, she smelled fresh hazelnut coffee brewing in the van. She felt a pang of envy, followed by guilt, as she imagined the steaming cup. I must not confuse my dislike of him with the fact that he has money, she thought.

The generator was buzzing at the tent, a small group of early risers huddled around the coffee urn. "I can see it's not ready yet," Rachel called out. "Do you think your warm bodies lurking around will make it brew any faster? Hi Pete, Kathy. Good to see you here." Familiarity developed from years of meeting at the rides, of sharing the disappointments and successes, however small, made for an open, friendly group.

"June, when did you get in?"

"Must have been around midnight. That hammer-headed nag of mine took her time about loading. Must have taken three hours to get her on. If she won't shape up, I'm going to have to look for another cayuse."

June's glittering humor-filled eyes told what a lie that was. Everyone there knew she would never part with her lovely chestnut Arabian mare. Somehow they made it to every ride on the circuit. The mare must be over twenty by now, and June was well into her sixties. They rode to finish, clocking up lifetime miles that were staggering. June was a tiny frail-looking woman with white hair cut very short, sticking out in wisps from under her Stetson. Her skin was weathered and wrinkled, and she was tougher than most. Many rookies made the mistake of trying to keep pace with her and Madge, the mare, only to be held at the rest stops for overextending their horses.

There followed a long discussion about how to load reluctant horses onto trailers. Someone finally noticed the coffee urn's lack of gurgling noises, and they pounced, styrofoam cups in hand. Things were starting to roll as the judges arrived in a jeep with the ride manager. By this time the sun was just breaking the horizon. As predicted, it looked to be a clear, crisp day. The coffee hounds moved off to their respective trailers, shouting hellos and in high spirits. Rachel passed people groggily coming out of tents, trailers, and the back of pickups. She stopped to chat a few times.

She found Margaret dressed, sitting propped up against her sleeping bag.

"I hope this coffee isn't too cold. I kept running into riders I know."

"Coffee in bed is such a treat I don't even care if it's stone cold." She was watching Kestrel framed in the open trailer doorway. The mare put her head down, quickly snatched a wisp of hay, then watched, chewing, as horses walked by on the way to be vetted. "It's like she's checking out the competition."

Kestrel's chewing reminded Rachel she had to force down her breakfast. "Sorry I don't have much here for you," she said as she peeled the egg. "Do you want half of this banana?"

"No, thanks. I'll get something in town."

"There are those hard little greasy doughnuts at the tent."

Margaret laughed. "You make them sound so appetizing."

Rachel changed out of her pajamas into sleek lycra electric-blue riding pants with leather set in the inside of the knees. After shyly turning away, she put on a racer-back bra and tank top, in soft sky blue. Over that she wore a silk long-sleeved undershirt, then a windbreaker. She slipped the rubber boots back on to save her riding shoes, high-tech running shoes with smooth soles and a heel.

"Let's go up for more coffee."

Just as they walked by Dwight's van, two young women started unloading the horses. A large bay gelding came charging out with his ears laid back. The woman on the end of the lead rope did her best to calm him, but Dwight's rough voice and abrupt unloading of a sweet but cowed black gelding came too soon for that. The bay reared slightly and ran back to the end of his lead. Dwight snatched the lead from his employee and gave it three vicious jerks.

"You can't let him get away with that," he said. Catching sight of Margaret and Rachel, who had paused to watch, he slipped into an oily heartiness. "Get his respect."

"There are other ways to gain respect from a horse," Margaret said distinctly.

"Stay out of this, honey."

"You do not have permission to call me honey," her cold angry voice rang out.

Watching on the sidelines, Rachel felt a soft glow of pride in Margaret. She fought down a beaming smile, not wishing to be openly insulting to Dwight. As Margaret turned away, however, she flashed a thumbs-up gesture.

He turned, astounded, to see their backs walking away. Word passed quickly around the grounds, and Margaret was identified as "Rachel's friend, the one who stood up to Dwight."

Drinking coffee, and eating a couple of the lethal doughnuts, they watched a few more horses go through their examinations. Rachel introduced Margaret to some of her friends, then left to get Kestrel ready.

When Dwight came up with his bay, he was sullenly silent and wouldn't look in Margaret's direction. What a baby, she thought. She admired the horse as he went through, strong and clean.

Rachel returned for the preride briefing, having left Kestrel tied to the trailer. She told Margaret she could get her a guest dinner ticket for the banquet if she wanted one. "We probably won't eat until about 7:00. The food on this ride is good, though."

Margaret listened in to the briefing, standing out as a non-rider among the fifty or so competitors. Almost immediately riders started leaving at thirty-second intervals. Each horse had eight-and-a-half hours to do the fifty miles, which translated to about a six-plus-mile-an-hour pace. Horses coming in late or early within a twenty-minute leeway were penalized. Keeping the pace was crucial to a competitive ride. Endurance riding, the Tevis Cup for example, was a flat-out race.

Margaret watched the horses timed out, some calm and efficient, others so tense they were barely controlled runaways. She could see her favorite team doing slow warm-ups while they waited their turn. "Number twenty-eight on deck," came the call. Rachel rode over, set her watch at noon to more easily figure elapsed time, and was timed out with "Go."

She waved back at Margaret, but Margaret could see that she was already focused on her ride and its strategy.

Margaret walked back to the truck. By the time she had changed into her conference clothes and driven through the grounds, the place had entirely emptied of horses. There was still some activity at the tent as workers scrambled for their cars and trucks to make the various rendezvous points ahead of the horses. Glancing at her watch, Margaret noticed that it was 8:30, barely time for breakfast if she hurried.

Nine

It had been a long day with all those male veterinarians, but as she pulled onto the Elkhorn Ranch grounds that evening Margaret was eager to see how Rachel had done on the ride. She spotted her almost immediately, lounging on the grass near the tent. Margaret parked the truck in the first place she could find, calling out as she neared Rachel, "How did it go?"

"Fine." The relaxed smile welcomed her. "We vetted through about twenty minutes ago." She patted the ground beside her. "How was your conference?"

"The best thing about it was that it was only one day."

Rachel grinned at her. "That bad?"

Noticing some stragglers cross the finish line, Rachel checked her watch. "Another five minutes and they would have been eliminated for going overtime."

Two of the horses bristled with equipment: high-tech packs, water bottles dangling, pouches hanging from every available attachment. Even a pouch sewn into the saddle pad was bulging. "Rookies," Rachel said.

"Why do you say that?" Margaret asked.

"Those horses are packing about twenty pounds of unnecessaries." She shook her head and grinned. "Didn't have any of that gear in the catalogs when I started. You have to trust ride management to supply the water and your lunch. Other than that, all you need is a sponge, a waist or cantle pack with a knife, cord, and small first-aid kit—and some way to stow your clothes as you peel them off through the day."

"I hadn't thought about the weight as being that critical."

"Oh, it is. When I train, I usually ride in chaps, use a stock saddle that weighs twenty-five pounds, and often have saddlebags with lunch and water strapped on. In competition I strip down to clothes that weigh five pounds maximum and use a seven-pound saddle. Kestrel's carrying about thirty-five or forty pounds less than she normally does. Rookies do it the other way around, pack all that gear just for the rides and the horse is suddenly bogged down with extra weight."

The man with the sorrel quarter horse very carefully and painfully dismounted, unable to stifle a whimper as he did so. He saw Margaret and smiled sheepishly at her. "Guess Ace and I have some learnin' to do." He turned to lead his tired horse away but stopped to stare at June, who strode up to Rachel and Margaret with her regular limber walk.

"I'm beat," she said as she plopped down beside them on the grass.

The man just shook his head, knowing what *beat* meant, and urged his reluctant horse back into a walk.

"Have a good ride, June?" Rachel asked.

"Super. Old crow bait made it through another one. How about you two? You looked very strong at the lunch stop. Going for the Tevis Cup this year, I hear."

"Yeah, I'm pretty excited. Kestrel breezed through the ride today. She's real close to being ready."

"Maybe I'll fly down to California and see you do it. Got an old friend I like to rustle up every so often." She turned to Margaret. "So what do you think of all this?"

"I think it's fascinating. It would be fun to work on these events. Maybe do some judging."

"Good idea to ride in a lot of rides if you want to do that. Always can use help at these things." June wiped her face with a red bandanna.

"So, anything new today at the conference?" Rachel explained briefly to June what Margaret had been doing that day.

"Oh, you're a vet." June looked at her assessingly. "Small animals?"

"No, large. Some of it was interesting. There was a good talk by an equine dentist. And some new theories about the cause of moon blindness."

They talked for a while, then Rachel and June left to check on their horses. When they returned, they saw only three more horses waiting to be checked through. One of them was Ace, a vastly different horse from earlier that day. The judges spent some time with Walter, the owner, answering his questions and offering some suggestions. There was a new respect and humility about him. As he left the judges, he stopped to talk with the group of women.

"I don't think this is Ace's sport," Walter said ruefully. "How much does one of these Arabs cost? Where did you get yours, Miss Duncan?"

"You can call me Rachel. I bred my mare. You can find a sound gelding for one or two thousand. Not all Arabs have what it takes, but a lot do. A mare, or any proven horse, will cost more, of course."

"You have any for sale?"

"I have some pretty good young horses coming along, and I can give you the names of other ranchers who will treat you right." She rose and walked to the nearby truck, took a card from the glove compartment, and wrote some names on the back.

Walter tucked it in his pocket. "I'll give you a buzz later this week, and thanks, Rachel," he shyly added.

She smiled. "You bet."

Hungry riders gathered, eyeing the tables covered with food. Roast beef, barbequed chicken, and—wonder of wonders—a concession to the vegetarians, a tofu enchilada casserole. Potato salad stood in iced bowls, and sliced tomatoes with sprigs of fresh basil on big blue-edged platters and huge bowls of garden salad waited. On a nearby table, arranged around the coffee urns, were peach pie, cakes, and mounds of fresh strawberries. Clearly enough to satisfy this hungry horde. Margaret ogled with the rest.

Finally, the dinner bell rang. During the meal everyone's peripheral attention was on the sequestered crew tallying up the scores. Coffee and pie were going down when the four-person-tent flap opened, and the workers were greeted with cheers and a scuffling for seats.

First the ride manager thanked the Elkhorn Ranch for the use of their land, then the vetting and recording teams and everyone else who made the ride work. Ribbons were given out to all those who completed the ride. Next came the awards for the divisions. Of the six placings in the lightweight division, June was in first with a score of ninety-seven.

By this time Margaret was on the edge of her chair. The names of the middleweight riders were read out, starting with sixth place. As they got to second place and Rachel's name still had not been called, she turned to Margaret with a funny grin and said, "I either did better or worse than I thought." Before Margaret could respond, they heard "First place goes to Rachel Duncan and Kestrel with a perfect score of one hundred."

Rachel's smile was broad as she threaded her way up to the announcer, surrounded by calls of "Pick up that Tevis Cup" and "Watch out, here she comes." On the way back to her seat amid backslaps and razzing, she was surprised to see Walter reach out and touch her arm like a talisman. "Good going, Rachel."

She laughed with pleasure and said, "You, next year."

"This feels like first place to me," he responded, holding up his hard-won completion ribbon.

Dwight Newton was second in the heavyweight division with a score of ninety-two. Margaret could just hear him complaining about the scoring that took off five points for the bit injury. "I'll bet the judge didn't look in every horse's mouth." He flicked an insinuating glance toward Rachel, but caught Margaret's eye instead. Her eyes, like the blue edge of an iceberg, froze him into silence. Rachel had seen nothing of this exchange.

The announcer quieted the buzz by holding up the blue wool horseblanket with Bitterroot Fifty emblazoned across the side. "The ride championship goes to Rachel Duncan on Kestrel."

Rachel folded it up, saying, "Thanks. Kestrel will look great in this."

"June Thorpe riding Madge is our reserve champion. Here are some shipping boots, June, to help speed up your travel time."

June went up to retrieve them, her eyes squinting as if the sun came straight into the tent. She croaked out, "Old flea bag will like these." Only the people sitting near could see the tears in her eyes. Turning her back to everyone, she took a while at the coffee urn. Margaret raised her eyebrows at Rachel.

"She knows that old horse doesn't have many miles left in her. This could be their last season together." Rachel's face took on the look of a sudden idea. "June might be a good one for Storm Queen. I'll have to get her up to the ranch and see how they get on."

"Matchmaker," Margaret said, her eyes a little damp, too.

Something turned over deep inside Rachel. She realized suddenly that she had been looking at Margaret a little too long. "Let's work our way back to the bedrolls."

"O.K.," Margaret said quietly.

They each went their own way, saying good night and exchanging addresses with some people. As they met outside the tent, Rachel declared, "I could use a hot bath tonight."

"Maybe there is something better." At Rachel's startled look, Margaret thought, My, our minds may be on similar paths. Aloud, she said, "I can give you a liniment rubdown."

Rachel, at that, looked only slightly less like a filly ready to bolt. "Umm" was her noncommittal reply.

Back at the trailer, Rachel took Kestrel's pulse again—a nice steady thirty beats a minute—then walked her around. She was loose and relaxed and eager for dinner. While Rachel was tending to the mare, Margaret was nest building, shaking out sleeping bags, sounding like a busy squirrel.

Rachel poked her head around the tailgate. "You all done in there?"

"Yes. Come in and get comfortable while I go to the outhouse one more time."

Rachel stood, bare feet on the bags, slowly slipping off her lycra tights. Her heart and thoughts were racing as she moved through the automatic routine of undressing. She stepped into the soft flannel pajamas, doing up the last button of the top as Margaret returned. Feeling tense and awkward, she sank down and started to crawl under the covers.

"No, don't get under the covers just yet. Lie on top." Margaret knelt down beside her. "Roll over on your stomach."

The heavy smell of liniment sharply filled the air, interlaced with an earthy, dusky aroma of fresh horse manure. Rachel felt her pajama top gently pushed up over the back of her neck, then shock—first cold, then hot—as the liniment and Margaret's hands reached her skin.

Rachel relaxed under the tender glowing touch, heat spreading over her body, following Margaret's hands. Lost in the afterglow of the liniment, she was never quite sure where they were. She felt the fatigue and fear drain away on a warm tide. She really didn't care when the ghastly maroon pajama bottoms were freed from her body and pushed to one side. The bunched muscles of thighs and calves loosened and melted. She felt hands discover her toes, the big pads and hollow arches. *Ahh, feet.* Those things at the end of the legs, so often forgotten and neglected. Now they felt like sea otter toes, spread out and floating.

With a jolt of alarm, she felt herself being turned over from the safety of her stomach. Dimly lit by the moon, Margaret was still real enough to bring Rachel back to the sense that the pleasure had come from this woman and not some ethereal otherness. Lying on her back, watching Margaret touch her, brought entirely new sensations to her. Now a whole body of tingling feelings swept after those hands, overcoming the liniment, leaving it behind. Rachel reached out to draw Margaret to her, wanting her whole body to feel more than hands, wanting the whole length of Margaret along her, breast to breast and breath warm on her face.

Their lips barely touched, the surface energy running along the edges so strong that anything more than the force of butterfly wings was too much. Beyond lips their bodies pushed against skin, trying to reach deep, to the center where everything was red, soft. Rachel was experiencing little brushes with panic intermingled with ease each time a new area was touched. "So this is how young horses feel," she murmured.

She felt the laughter through Margaret's rib cage and her lips along the edge of her ear as she whispered back, "Yes. You are my filly to gentle with sweet talk and rubdowns."

"Humhgummmn." Rachel nuzzled into Margaret's shoulder, then gave her a little nip.

"I can see you will take some taming." Margaret stroked Rachel's breasts, the nipples standing hard like the chestnuts on the inside of a horse's legs. She licked with wide flat horse tongues along Rachel's hipbones to the inside of her thighs.

"Achh." She spat. "I forgot about the liniment."

Roaring with laughter, they rocked each other. Soon they swam deep together. Neither one could tell if she were the one giving or experiencing the feeling. It was an uncharted sea for Rachel, a familiar cove for Margaret. Rachel found her whole body in harmony with her same species, made even more familiar by the womanness. This connectedness had only come to her before through the flesh and spirit of a horse. To feel the combined dance, the ready willing firmness and power between her legs, minds and bodies communicating on a plane that defied description. Rachel had had a dream once, that Kestrel made love to her, the mare hovering over her, desire flooding out of her eyes. There had been no touch. None was needed. The passion was thick and palpable.

She checked to see if this mane fanned out across her stomach, the last ripple lapping at her breasts, was grey or gold. It was hard to tell in the moonlight.

"Margaret?"

"Yes, love."

"I felt lost for a moment. Hold me."

Time and passion ebbed, the two women held each other under the high curved vault of the horse trailer, allowing Rachel a pause to absorb the flood of feelings and sensations which had swamped her. Margaret held her and rocked her and crooned wordless things. Rachel fell asleep, content.

In the morning she woke to the memory and reached for Margaret, softly snoring at her side. Caressing her awake, cherishing the lovely lovingness of her, Rachel found herself starting to cry. She tried to stop, but couldn't. She was too open to close herself. There were no body-wracking sobs, just slow tears leaking out, it felt, from her stomach, her heart, from all the lonely places long lying out of reach of her awareness. Long-defended sad places had been reached by Margaret's loving touch.

"Tell me, love."

It was hard, as usual, for Rachel to put her feelings into words, to try to express the sadness of so many years, good years most of them, that had been missing this closeness. "You know, I was happy, basically. I knew I wouldn't fit into being married. The experience I had when I was young. . .well, I thought I had grown out of it." She told Margaret about Amy then, and Margaret wasn't surprised to hear it. "But how likely would it be for me to meet a woman like you?"

Margaret chuckled. "Not very likely with one person for every twenty square miles, and most of those in the cities, and half of those men."

At this point Kestrel lost her patience and started pawing at the ramp, whoofling her nose into the trailer. She grabbed Rachel's blanket, giving it a yank.

"My other lady calls."

Margaret watched Rachel stand up, naked this time, to get the feed ready. It was her first unobstructed view of the body she had felt in the dark, under her, with liniment-tingling hands. The smooth upper body with amazingly developed shoulders had long, flat, clearly defined muscles that ran on down her arms to her big long-fingered hands. Her breasts were not even large enough to hang, but Margaret remembered their soft round sweetness. The muscles along her lower back and her tight, small, almost-square buttocks made it seem as if she had no waist. Her thighs and calves would have made any Wimbledon player chartreuse with envy.

"Do you run?" Margaret asked.

"Huh?"

"Run. Do you?"

"Oh, yes. I go about four miles five times a week. Have to for the endurance rides. On those you can get off and run beside your horse to give them a break. On steep hills, I get off, grab her tail, and let my horse pull me up. Why?"

"I was just admiring your lovely legs."

"Where are your lovely legs?" A flush of desire made her voice husky. Rachel pulled off the sleeping bag tucked up under Margaret's arms. Her knees collapsed at the sight of Margaret, and she fell across her, giggling like a schoolgirl.

A deep male voice called out, "Aren't you girls up yet?"

"That you, Pete?"

"Yeah. Jane and I wondered if you want to go out to breakfast with us."

"Sure." Too late Rachel raised her eyebrows at Margaret, who gave her a playfully fierce exasperated look.

"Won't be long," she called out to Pete and then whispered to Margaret, her lips brushing her cheek as she spoke. "Can you stay with me tonight?"

"I'll have to check with my answering service to see if there are no other alluring offers," Margaret teased. "Like forty horses with colic."

She kissed Rachel. "I'd love to stay."

Ten

I t was a slow drive back. Overpowering desire drew Rachel's attention to the lovely glowing woman sitting next to her. She drove slowly, her body vibrating. Cars honked and sped past, with more than their usual irritation at being behind a horse trailer. Every not-too-conspicuous place she would pull over, ostensibly so the cars could pass, but really to soak up the image of Margaret.

"We are never going to get back at this rate," Rachel laughed, pulling out again.

"At least I can just sit here and look at you," Margaret teased.

"How about you doing the driving?"

"Oh, no. Don't be so cruel," Margaret pleaded. "I want to learn every eyebrow movement, every hair on your chin"—Rachel snorted—"the way the edge of your nose curves to your lip." Her voice got deep. "I want to imagine those lips searching me out, those strong hands on the steering wheel taking me places."

By this time Rachel's breathing was short and rapid. She could feel the warm juiciness of her pants under her jeans. "Talk about cruel. You had better mind your manners," she said, making a great effort at sternness.

Just then the right-side tires bumped off the rim of the pavement. Rachel could feel the trailer follow the truck then swerve back as she pulled the steering wheel over. Sobering up fast, she swore, "Damn, you are one sure fire-driving hazard, lady."

The afternoon light played across Rachel's face, silhouetting her rugged profile, the Crazy Woman mountains a suitable backdrop. Margaret caught a tantalizing glance from Rachel, whose lips softened in a smile as her tongue dampened them.

With great effort, they managed to pull in at the ranch late in the day. While Margaret checked in with her answering service, Rachel unloaded Kestrel. Kate came up and eagerly asked, "How was it?"

Rachel turned with a blissfully happy face and said, "Oh, wonderful."

"How did you place? Kestrel looks great."

Rachel turned with a slightly puzzled look at her mare. "I forgot. We won. No points off. Ride champion, too."

"You forgot?" A small smile tugged at the corners of Kate's mouth.

Margaret came out of the door and down the steps. "No pressing calls. I can stay the—" She saw it all in a flash: Rachel's scarlet face, Kate's by this time ear-to-ear grin. She smiled, too. "Hi, Kate."

Rachel was busy taking the shipping boots off the mare. When she stood up, Kate took the boots and lead line from her. "I know you must be hungry. I can manage here. 'Night," she sang out, leading Kestrel away.

As soon as they were inside, Rachel said, "I'm not hungry."

"Oh, but I am." Margaret walked saucily to the refrigerator. She opened the door and threw a raised eyebrow at Rachel.

Rachel leaned against the doorjamb to the living room. She hooked her thumb in the corner of her pocket and softly drawled out, "I'm getting more hungry. Maybe I will have something to eat." She watched Margaret's face and saw a little edge of disappointment. "I think I'll start with toes, or maybe a juicy thigh."

Margaret shrieked as Rachel swept her up in her arms and carried her across the living room floor to the big bedroom with the evening light coming in through the windows. She struggled some, not fiercely, just enough to add drama. Dumped on the bed with the carved cherry headboard red in the light, she watched Rachel take off her dusty jacket.

"Now I am going to get you ready to eat." She peeled Margaret like the delectable exotic fruit she was, tissue-paper-wrapped from a crate that had seemed to take forever in the shipping. As more of Margaret was uncovered, Rachel slowed, becoming more serious. She knelt back on the patchwork quilt.

"What a lovely woman you are."

She removed the rubber band holding the yellow braid, then fanned the hair out on the pillow like a halo from a Renaissance painting. The sunset light angled in, flickering red-and-yellow flashes across Margaret's hair. "Your hair is like the Yellowstone River, the water flowing over the gold on the riverbed."

Running her fingers through the ripples of Margaret's hair, she brought up a handful and breathed deeply of it. "I want to know your scent, what pleases you."

"You please me." Margaret felt a sense of newness, of being discovered. She was not just bringing a body to Rachel with herself as an afterthought. She felt whole in a way she hadn't experienced before. Most women had taken her beauty as a prize, then, after showing her off, had not known what to do, who she was. By this tentative woman she felt seen.

Passion overcame them both. Rachel found the power that comes with lovemaking. Margaret guided her over the trail of her body. Rachel slid one finger into the rich valley of Margaret's vagina, feeling for the first time the complexity of her own interior. The lips at the door, the folds and ridges, the round, taut cervix deep inside. "You won't hurt me," Margaret's voice reached her. "Turn your palm up, and there is room for two or three fingers. You can rest your chin on your palm and put your lips to my clitoris."

Rachel was relieved to hear what to do. She felt like a new foal trying to find her legs in the straw. She had always heard the taste of a woman described as salty. The juices which flowed around her lips and hand were mildly sweet, though, not like flowers, exactly, more body, perhaps like new-mown hay, light and fresh in the field.

Her passion built with Margaret's. She felt a breathless power holding this woman she loved between her mouth and her hand. Remembering how she had disliked the in and out driving jabs of a penis, she held Margaret steady with her hand, only occasionally pressing deep, then curling the tip of her fingers against the ribbed roof of the chamber.

Margaret's breathing, moving body climaxed, then Rachel felt tugging ripples pulling against her fingers. For a while she lay over Margaret, her fingers still holding her on the inside. A beach-comber on the ebb tide.

In the shower they lovingly soaped each other's spent bod-ies, their muscles loose, satisfied. The touch of the soap bar left trails of excitement, tingling reminders of their passion.

Rachel gave Margaret the terrycloth robe and found another pair of her father's pajamas, this one blue-and-grey stripes.

"Quite a collection," Margaret said, eyeing them. "Where do your pajamas come from?"

"They were my dad's. Seems a shame not to use them."

"That's a matter of opinion."

Rachel looked down, held the legs out like a skirt, glanced up at Margaret, and burst into laughter. "You may have a point."

After throwing together something to eat and ravenously starting in on it, their appetites dissolved into each other's eyes. Giving up on food they curled up on the sofa with tea-filled mugs in their hands. Rachel had lit a fire in the Minerva fireplace, its warmth mirroring their own.

Margaret asked about Rachel's family. "I know nothing about your past. To me you are sprung up from the sagebrush full-blown."

"It's a long story."

"I'm not going anyplace, and I want to hear."

"O.K." Rachel stared in silence at the fire for a while. Mar-garet did not push her.

"I was born here." She tilted her head toward the bedroom and smiled softly. "In that bed." Rachel took a sip of tea. "My mother, Mildred, grew up in Boston. Summered in the Adiron-dacks. Old money, you know? She met my father, Leslie Dun-can, through her brother Jack. They both went to the Univer-sity of Montana, Dad for the agriculture and Jack for the ropes courses, the mountaineering school there. He was a bit of a fa-natic. Managed to get swept off the face of a mountain by an av-alanche before he was thirty." She paused, trying to reconstruct the wiry man with a casual air from her child memory.

"Anyway, Jack took Leslie home with him one spring break. Said it was time he tasted real maple syrup." She laughed, remembering this piece of family trivia. "Well, the upshot of that visit was that Mother dropped out of Sarah Lawrence, flew out to Missoula, and waitressed until Leslie graduated a few months later. Then they got married. My grandparents were so mad she married a "cowboy" that they wouldn't come to the wedding, gave her no dowry, and would never visit the ranch.

"When I was about seven, I guess, Mother took me east with her when Grandmother had an operation. I felt awkward and clumsy, disapproved of, in the way. I tell you, it was a relief to get home and put on my blue jeans and T-shirts again. That was the only time I ever met them." Rachel got up to put another piece of applewood on the fire.

"My father was a real charmer," she said, her back to Margaret, staring into the fire. Softly, she added, "What's known as a lady-killer." She was quiet for a while. Margaret didn't prod her to continue, just let her alone, but when Rachel finally turned to sit next to her, Margaret reached gently for her hand. With her palm held up, she held Rachel's hand as if it were a very fragile flower or wounded young animal, with no grip so Rachel could leave if she wanted.

"When I was little, Dad spent a lot of time with me. Took me to town on the big front seat of the truck. He was so handsome, and I was proud to be his daughter. He took me on a pack trip to the Crazy Woman Mountains when I was eight. We fished for trout and ate them 'most every morning, fried, crispy with corn-meal breading." She looked over at Margaret, tears in her eyes. "It's funny the things that stand out."

Margaret nodded with a kind look in her eyes, not saying anything.

"This is hard to talk about," Rachel admitted.

"You are doing just fine."

"He taught me just about everything I know about horses, you know? He was real hard to please, a perfectionist from the get-go. Didn't know the meaning of *I can't*. Saw any horse or human that couldn't match his standards as weak or puny. I just learned how to try harder, 'til one day I quit caring whether I pleased him or not.

"It must have been hard on my mother. I think she may have tried to be a buffer for his harshness. I imagine when they first got married that they loved each other. But when I was around nine, Dad just sort of disappeared. He'd come home after I was in bed, he was silent at breakfast, hard to catch up with. I didn't know it then, but he had started drinking a lot and was fooling around with other women. Mom tried extra hard to look good, I think. She was never fat, but was always dieting and worried looking. I didn't understand until years later how Dad's fooling around made her feel so bad about herself, like somehow it was her fault."

Margaret nodded again, her experience with Trudy giving her real understanding of what Rachel meant.

"I wish we had been closer. I kind of blamed her for Dad being so unhappy. I think, really, she got the blame from all of us, herself included. She gave me of herself in ways I didn't see until later. Like my love of classical music. Mother had a tenderness, too, with animals that Dad didn't really have. She had a border collie, Scout, that she loved." Rachel laughed, remembering the way Scout would take your hand gently in her mouth to lead you somewhere, or grasp the edge of her mother's skirt to urge a walk.

"Talk about sibling rivalry. I swear that dog was my sister in my mother's eyes." Rachel squirmed, got up. "Want some more tea or something? You don't really want to hear all this, do you? There really is not a lot more."

Margaret could sense evasion at work. Firmly, she said, "Sit down and tell me the rest. I want to know your past. Tea can wait."

Rachel complied. "When I was sixteen, Mother went to a doctor for tranquilizers. That night, after Dad went out and I had gone to bed, she drove the car down to the cattle guard, turned it off but left the lights on. She must have wanted to be sure that Dad found her, and not me. She took all those pills and washed them down with a pint of whiskey. I guess it was the only way she thought she could get through to him about how bad she had been hurting. I still wish she had gotten herself to a good therapist instead of to that doctor," Rachel said with deep sadness.

She stood again to poke the fire. When she turned, the light from below changed her face to a strange mask. "I've never told this to anyone before, except a counselor I saw a few years ago."

She sat back down, drawing her knees up to her chin and wrapping her arms around them. "It was a late night for him. By the time he came down the driveway, Mother's car battery was dead. And so was she. Dad was pretty drunk. He couldn't stop in time. Plowed into the car. He thought he had killed her. He shook me awake at three in the morning. I thought he was angry with me for not being up to do the chores. Then I saw the time. He was crying a lot, and it was hard to make out what he was saying. I called an ambulance. When they got here, they called the sheriff.

"Everybody tried to keep what really happened from me. It was ruled a suicide. The grief and shame broke my father. Jane Hamilton, a friend of my mother's, came in days to see to things until I was through high school. She was upset that she hadn't been able to help Mildred more. Dad never left the ranch again after the funeral. Jim was there, did most of the work around the ranch and the town errands.

"The week of my high school graduation Dad had a stroke. College was out for me then, so I used the money I had saved up for it and bought the cattle. I had to take care of him, but the herd gave me a good excuse to get away from the house once in a while. He just sat in his wheelchair and cried for four years. I never could bring myself to comfort him, even if it might have helped. He was an old man at forty-eight. One day he just died of another stroke. So there I was, twenty-two years old, with a ranch to run." She stopped and looked thoughtful. "Kate's age." She shook her head, appreciating perhaps for the first time what she had accomplished.

"Boy, did I run. I kept myself so busy, I ran myself into the ground. One day Jane suggested I might need to talk with someone who could help me put my past to rest. She gave me the name of a therapist in Lewiston." She looked at Margaret. "You have to understand that the idea of seeing a psychologist in this part of the country means that you are crazy. . .insane."

"Sounds like you would have been crazy not to."

"Yeah, well, I only figured that out later. It took me a few more years to get myself to this woman Martha. I saw her about three years as it turned out. At first I thought I'd go two or three times, she'd explain it all to me, fix me up, and that would be that." Rachel grinned ruefully.

"She helped me realize how my parents' problems were their own, not anything I did or didn't do. It was a relief. I finally cried about losing them, but I think I was still scared about getting close to anyone." She looked at the loving woman sitting beside her. "I am now. I try not to think about losing you."

Margaret responded intensely. "Rachel, I'm scared too. I didn't think I was willing to take the risk again, but I can see that I am. What happens between us is only ours. Nobody else's, past or present. We'll just have to do the best we can." Margaret gently drew Rachel to her, to soothe away the tightness that telling her story had brought to Rachel. "Thank you for telling me," Margaret said, her lips moving to Rachel's hair. "I know it was hard."

With the gift of Rachel's story, deep from the past, the present seemed richer, fuller, to both of them.

During the month of June, Rachel concentrated on keeping Kestrel fit without overtiring her. She tuned herself to the mare's keenness, playing her like a sweet country fiddle. Two weeks before the Tevis she gave her the freedom of the range with the other horses. She brought her in only once to check on her and have the blacksmith put on new shoes.

They were ready. Margaret would come with them. She had already made arrangements with Dr. McCoy to cover each other's emergency calls. He was delighted to do this for her; it meant he could take his long dreamed of deep-sea fishing trip. Kate was bouncing off her toes with excitement. They would begin the thousand-mile trip on a Wednesday, taking two days, and then end with a short one-hundred-fifty-mile drive Friday, arriving early for the vetting. The dream was coming close to becoming a reality. The Tevis Cup.

Eleven

The four females were on the road early Wednesday morning. Kestrel, loaded with her breakfast hay, was the only calm one in the bunch. The setting moon gave a cold steel edge to the sharp alpine ridges of the Crazy Woman Mountains. In the hours before dawn, the women passed the time talking about the coming race.

"Two years ago I rode the trail on a four-day clinic led by the woman who won the Tevis Cup that year. I'll tell you, it's a rugged piece of work," Rachel said as she pulled on to I-90 at Big Timber. "Wendell Robie, who started the ride in 1955, claims there never has been a Tevis Cup rider lost for more than two days." Both Kate and Rachel roared with laughter. Margaret, sitting between the two of them, found herself looking back and forth, wondering what the hell was so funny.

"There is real danger, isn't there? Tell me," she demanded, looking scared. "All of it."

"Most of the country is accessible only by foot, horseback, or helicopter—" Rachel was interrupted by Kate's snort of laughter.

"I know you both think this is very funny, but I'm beginning to wonder about your sanity."

"Well, there is an emergency helicopter, and the local search-and-rescue mounted patrol is on hand. They sort of keep track of the riders."

"Sort of?"

"No, they do. They keep pretty close tabs on everyone. If you drop out and don't inform an official, they won't ever let you ride in the Tevis Cup again."

"Sounds like a really harsh punishment," Margaret said.

Rachel, totally agreeing with her, caught no hint of sarcasm. She went on. "Progress reports are posted for the riders' crews, relayed by radio, so they will know who's still in the race."

"Yes?" Margaret said on an up-note.

A wild fire in her eyes, Kate took up the story. "There's rattlesnakes and bear and mountain lions, according to June. And giardia from the beaver poop, so you can't drink any of the water."

Margaret looked seriously at Kate. "You mean she's entirely dependent on the ride organization to supply her?"

"Yes," Rachel answered. "And the temperatures range between 40 and 120 degrees." Her eyes were shining.

Margaret was beginning to see that Rachel wanted, welcomed, and was invigorated by the whole challenge. Not just the miles, but the hardships as well, the test. "You both love the danger of this, don't you?" she exclaimed. "This must be akin to sky-diving."

The fan of wrinkles around Rachel's eyes deepened. "That's true. The trail does go pretty high, close to nine thousand feet. Altitude sickness is another hazard. I doubt I'll have any problems, but it does take its toll on the flatlanders."

"It's the ultimate," Kate said. "I'm really glad I get this chance to crew. Someday I want to do the race myself."

Margaret shook her head. "I guess it's the Olympics of your sport. It seems a terrible ordeal to me, for both horses and riders."

"That's true," Rachel said, sobered. "The experienced riders know when to quit—usually—and the P&R teams at the ten checkpoints ensure that the horses which should be pulled are. If you are smart, you never exceed your own or your horse's capacity."

"What's to keep riders from pushing their horses too hard?" Margaret asked.

"For one thing, let's hope, common sense. No competition is worth a good horse. And, secondly, if you want top-ten placing, your horse must be fit to go on, even after the thirty-minute final check. The Haggin Award is presented to the horse finishing in the top ten in the best condition."

Margaret sat back, sandwiched between her two companions. "What have I gotten myself into?" she asked. "Aiding and abetting maniacs." She looked right and left. A Cheshire-cat grin greeted her on each side. She rolled her eyes and said, "I guess I'm stuck with the two of you."

"I hope so," Rachel said, with a look of impish innocence.

The three women rode quietly for a while. Kate, resting her forehead against the cool glass, watched the island of sharp peaks nicknamed the Crazies. Margaret solemnly noted the far-off Beartooth Mountains become overlaid with the mighty Absarokas, their sharp combined teeth snarling to guard Yellowstone Park at their backs. Just after Butte, they took I-15 south. A half-circle wall of mountain faced them, named mundanely the Butte Highlands. She looked out the window with her mouth slightly open in awe. Huge mountain ranges had been passed that day, the Absorokas, Bridgers, Tobacco Roots, Spanish Peaks. They rose up from the prairie and kept on going into the sky. The snow on the peaks tried to pass for clouds. It truly needed to be Big Sky Country to hold all these shouldering, elbowing giants.

"I-15 doesn't get a whole lot of traffic," Rachel said.

This Margaret could easily believe. In the last hour they had seen three cars, one truck, and at least fifty antelope grazing on the rolling velvety soft brown hills. As Rachel exited at the town of Monida, she said, "We get to save Monida Pass 'til first thing tomorrow." The truck whined down through the gears and rattled across the cattle guard. "June's ranch is in Lakeview. She's putting us up for the night."

The house that June stepped out of was startlingly modern. Dug into the bank overlooking Red Rock Lakes, it was made of the lakes' namesake. Stone walls flowed in a long curve from the hillside. All one story, it was roofed with cedar shakes, and had an earthy, connected-to-the-ground look about it.

The stables were reached by walking under a grape arbor, a cool tunnel of leaves and dangling fruit. Kestrel, turned out into a roomy corral, trotted the boundary, called out to Madge, June's mare, then buckled down to the soft dirt for a long, satisfying roll. She grunted, rose and shook herself, then settled down to steady grazing.

"I wouldn't mind doing some of that myself," Rachel said with a grin to June.

"I didn't think to pick some grass for you, but maybe a salad would do instead." June led them to the house. "There's a chicken in the oven, too."

During dinner Kate noticed a bundle on a rawhide string around Margaret's neck. Her eyes kept going back to it until Margaret became aware of Kate's curiosity.

"This is my prayer bag. I brought it with me to help on the ride." Then she proceeded to describe the bag's origins: a workshop on reconnecting to the Earth Mother through Indian and animal spirits.

Kate grunted her aknowledgment.

Dinner conversation swept on around them. After dinner June announced, "I have a treat for you."

Margaret patted her stomach. "I don't think I could eat dessert. That was a great dinner."

June laughed. "I thought I'd save dessert until later. This treat isn't edible. Come on."

June led them along a long winding path to the lake. "Be real quiet now," she warned. "Look over there." She pointed at a two-story beaver lodge. A huge nest had been built on top of it, and soon the architect floated regally into view. A pristine white trumpeter swan with a black bandit bill mask rose up out of the water, stood her full height, and flapped her seven-foot wingspread. Moving like Queen Victoria in her later years, she reached the top of her nest and settled down on her eggs with a wiggle to tuck them in.

Kate breathed out a soft, "Wow."

Margaret said very quietly, "She is beautiful. I have never seen anything like this, just the swans in zoos."

"Follow me," June whispered.

Continuing on the trail around the edge of the lake, June told them that this was a wildlife refuge, one of the few places outside Alaska that the trumpeter swans were found. "Because of the hot springs here, the swans are year-round residents. They were at the brink of extinction back in 1912, when a small group was discovered here. At that time only sixty-eight were known to exist in the wild. This refuge was established in 1935, and now there are about three hundred on the lakes."

Near a small cove they came within sight of two swans, who mate for life, sharing child care. Five grey cygnets scurried their baby legs to keep up with the pace of their giant parents.

"We were lucky today," June said.

Her guests smiled their pleased agreement.

Returning another way, they came upon a small runway with a little Piper Cub parked in a hangar. "Is this yours?" Margaret asked.

"Yes. I got tired of driving these damn mountains every time I needed something more complex than a can of soup. Takes me less than an hour now to get to Pocatello or Butte."

Margaret was impressed. "Pretty neat."

" 'Course, the wind and weather keep me grounded a lot, but I just work around that."

"Can't haul a horse trailer with one, though," Kate said.

"I'm working on it," June allowed.

Their slow walk back brought them out above the house. Just the roof was visible, blending in with the shape of the land. Kestrel threw up her head when she saw Rachel, calling a deep whicker to welcome her back. "Don't worry, gal. I won't go off and leave you," Rachel answered.

Rachel slid through the poles of the fence to spend some time with her mare. Kate and June chatted their way into the house, devising flying horse trailers, while Margaret sat out on a low rim of rock to merge with the serene stately mountains. The air went on forever, tinged with orange as the sun neared the mountain's edge. The sky was huge between grand craggy masses of rock and snow, and Margaret felt herself as small as an ant, only an animal guest there. She thought about the swans and felt their fragility. It reminded her of her own. She watched the sun's loss as it slowly gave up its light with a struggle fought in colors.

Margaret stood to face the last of the sun, her back dark with night, her front a warm reddish glow. Her voice rose in a singing Sioux chant to the setting sun, her arms accenting the words.

She did not see Kate, who had come out to the patio to watch the sunset. Instead, she watched Margaret. When Rachel showed up Kate slipped back inside.

Margaret felt Rachel come near, then gather her up in warm arms. "Sweet woman," Rachel said, "why are you standing out here in the dark?"

"I have just seen a sunset." Margaret snuggled close to Rachel. "It felt like my first one. Almost as if I were a participant."

"Yes. The silence, the quiet vastness of these mountains calms me." Rachel stood close to Margaret, their bodies lightly touching. "I'm feeling a little tense now, though." She gave Margaret a nuzzling soft kiss. "Let's see if we are lucky enough to have our own room."

They were. A queen-sized bed greeted them as June showed them in. Next to it a porcelain bowl held peonies, both light whitish pink and a deeper lusty pink. When they were alone, Rachel put her hand out to cover one of the flowers. Her fingers delicately explored its petals. She found Margaret watching her. "These feel like you do inside."

Suspended in the act of turning down the bed covers, Margaret felt the slow opening of desire running in like a spring tide. She walked around the bed, her eyes staying on Rachel's. "Let's shower."

The simple motions of undressing each other seemed to remove each layer of fatigue. Clothes pooled around their feet. The warmth of bare skin felt electric. Breasts seemed to reach for each other's roundness, finding hollows to fit into where none appeared to exist.

Once they had reluctantly covered each other with bathrobes, Rachel opened the bedroom door to the hall. "Coast is clear," she whispered. Holding hands they ran tiptoeing down the hall. Giggling wildly they piled up at the bathroom door, Margaret sinking down, into a crouch, holding her knees.

The sexual energy quickly changed from laughter to silent intensity. Hands made soapy paths over the skin. Rachel's rough hands slipped easily over Margaret's normally sheltered areas. She reveled in the softness, the curves, of Margaret's smooth body. Rachel followed the flows of breasts, waist, hips, thighs. An image entered her mind, and she spoke to her lover of it.

"You haven't been here yet for a winter, but I just had this memory. It's how you feel to my hands." She held Margaret full against her, leaning into the shower's wall, the water a hot rain flowing over them. "In the fall, after the wheat is cut, the long stubble is golden, and when it snows the white lies beneath it. The shape of the rolling plains comes through, for miles, with the yellow glow suspended above, like fine hair."

"Hmmm," Margaret murmured against Rachel's neck. They kissed, with tongues as warm as the water flowing over their shoulders. Four nipples, hard from arousal, surfaced through water running around them like boulders in a stream.

"Are you rinsed in all the crucial places?"

"Yes," Rachel said, with a shy smile.

Margaret then pushed the lever to *off*, reached out the shower door for her towel, and with more urgency than with the soap, applied herself to drying off. Rachel left her shy attack in the shower stall and within seconds the mood became a race with the bed as the finish line.

The sheets felt cold, their hurriedly dried bodies making wet patches over them. Pushing back the sheet and wool blanket, Rachel ran the tips of two fingers along Margaret's cheek to the firm edge where her lips met. The soft journey took her along the collar bone to the long curve of breast. Her mouth closed over Margaret's nipple like a hungry sea anemone. Margaret felt Rachel's leg wrap over her hip, the inside surface slippery from liquid of her own making.

Rachel's voice, softly vibrating against Margaret, reached her by way of her skin as well as sound. "You feel so good," Rachel said, running her hands, wide open, with every fingerprint whorl reading Margaret's body. "You are so smooth, one area flowing into the next. So different from men."

"Yes. I've never been with a man. . .but I can imagine."

Rachel moved around so she could kiss Margaret on the mouth. As her passion grew her motions became insistent, rhythmically pushing against Margaret.

"Whoa, baby," Margaret stroked her lover's cheek with her hand, softly pushing her away. "Let's kiss together. Play with our tongues. Dance our lips."

Her lips brushed lightly across Rachel's eyelids, forehead, to the corners of her mouth. There, her tongue came out lizardlike to taste the air, tease the field of energy surrounding Rachel's lips. Margaret slid on top of her lover, her full weight fitting their bodies tightly together. Hands flat on the bed, Margaret drew her long hair back and forth lightly across Rachel's shoulders, breasts, stomach. Occasionally her nipples would brush across Rachel's heightened body, shocking her in their firm contrast. Then she rose up to ride astride.

Rachel felt the warm suck of Margaret's vagina pulling at her lower belly and felt her own clitoris rising to meet that sweet place. Very slowly the slippery lips rocked over the hard muscles of her abdomen.

As she rode, Margaret reached behind her buttocks to find Rachel's clitoris among the wet folds. The swollen form near the loosely draped opening reached for her fingers. Wanting her tongue and lips to exchange places with her hand, Margaret turned around. Her own vagina left a snail-like trail behind, as she slid over Rachel's belly, then breasts, making an offering to her lover's mouth.

At first Rachel felt distracted. Her focus moved from her lips and tongue buried deep, finding Margaret's clitoris, to that of her own being searched out. Then it all shifted. All the sensations in her body and mind blended. The boundaries erased. It could have been her own eager mouth lightly nuzzling her clitoris.

The orgasm that welled up to push all the tension out of her body, letting pleasure ride into the empty space, surprised Rachel. Only briefly did she drift, suspended, before she became aware of Margaret, still near her peak.

Margaret turned around, rested her hands on the bedstead, then again lowered herself within range of Rachel's mouth. The intensity suddenly doubled when she felt first, not Rachel's tongue, but her finger slipping deep and powerful into her vagina, followed by the firm circle of mouth surrounding Margaret's clitoris.

Moans escaped to be contained by the bedroom walls. Finally, as their bodies stilled long enough to let sleep enter, they lay tightly interwoven in the middle of the queen-sized bed.

Monida Pass, elevation 6,870 feet, and with it the Continental Divide, was behind them by nine the next morning. Typical of many Montana passes, it crept up on you in long steady uphill climbs, a cool change of air at the top the only tangible sign of a summit. On the right the Bitterroot Mountains acted as separation between Idaho and Montana. Now the curve of the Snake River escorted them across the big, flat potato and lava fields of southeastern Idaho, and way off to the east the unmistakable Tetons pushed their turgid nipples into the sky. Herds of sentinel antelope flashed their white rumps every so often. At Twin Falls, they turned south on 93 to have Nevada welcome them with the town of Jackpot.

The sign, Winnemucca, Pop. 4140, greeted them after a long day. The main drag, with its raucous fast-food restaurants and gas stations, sprouted one-armed bandits in the least likely places. Rachel turned west on a road that rapidly changed to dirt. About a mile out of town, she pulled up to a funky pink stucco motel. In the back were corrals with corrugated metal sunscreens. A single spindly tree grew by the door, so bereft of leaves it was difficult to make out its species.

"All it lacks is a pink plastic flamingo," Rachel boasted.

"How did you find this place?" Margaret asked.

"Word of mouth from other horse travelers." Rachel got out of the truck, stretched, and rang the buzzer. A middle-aged woman, very short and slightly plump, her hair in pin curlers, opened the door. "Come in. I'll be back in a sec."

While they waited, Margaret and Kate were captivated by the photographs taped up all over the walls. There were snapshots of winning Thoroughbreds at every track in the country, each with a different jockey. "Why are these here?" Kate asked, finding no common theme.

"Dotty can tell you," Rachel answered.

The little woman came back from her living quarters, still fluffing out her hair. "Everyone wants to know, or leastways most. I used to exercise racehorses, breezed them and all. Those are pictures of the horses I rode."

"But why aren't you riding any of them in the races?" asked Kate.

Dotty looked at her, saw her youth, then answered patiently. "In those days girls did all the behind-the-scenes work and got none of the limelight. They said we couldn't ride in races because we weren't strong enough. Of course, that overlooked the fact that it was the gals who got those rambunctious fillies and colts shook down enough so the boys could handle them." Even though Dotty winked and grinned at Kate, the younger woman could see that the unfairness had been like sandpaper to her life.

"Just got the one old crippled mare now. She broke her leg in a race, and the owners wanted to put her down. I begged them off. After I nursed her back to her feet again, I bought this motel, built the corrals. Been here ever since."

She went out with them to show where Kestrel should be put. The Thoroughbred neighed a greeting to her night's companion. "She doesn't get many visitors. I bought that goat for her, but she won't give it the time of day."

Later that evening, Margaret studied the map of Nevada as she stretched out across the double bed in the motel room. It was about time to turn in, so Kate was gathering her things together to go to her room.

"Just look at this!" Margaret sat up, outrage in her voice. "The Indian reservations are these tiny postage stamps, and look," she jabbed her finger as she pointed, "here beside Walker Indian Reservation is a square marked Danger Area. I wonder if it's a military toxic waste dump. The wildlife refuges are as small and few as the Indian lands, but look at these gigantic benignly named places. Cactus Range, Belted Range, Pintwater Range, and Sheep Range. These are all military bombing test areas, and they are monstrously huge." Her eyes flashed. "You can certainly tell where our country's priorities are."

Kate shrugged. "It's an old story. But the size of the reservation doesn't relate to the freedom, or the self-determination, just to the size of the pen."

Margaret quietly folded the map. She looked at Kate, her eyes puzzled. "I'd think tribal lands would be vital to the life of the tribe."

"Yes, of course they are." Kate picked up her backpack and tugged back and forth with one of the zippers. In a clear, firm voice, she said, "It's the theft and commercialization of our spirituality that I have trouble with."

"What do you mean?" Margaret asked. Not waiting for a response, she continued, "There is a powerful move in the country to follow Indian spiritual practices."

Kate's face was showing her growing discomfort. She seemed to appeal to Rachel with her eyes, then said, "Margaret, this is uneven ground for us to walk. Maybe you and Rachel could break up some clods." She shouldered her pack and with her hand on the doorknob said, "Sweet dreams."

Margaret stared at the door, not focusing, then looked at Rachel. "What is she talking about?" Her growing righteous indignation made it clear she wasn't really interested in an answer. "Is Kate telling me that I shouldn't honor and respect the Indian teachings about the environment and connectedness to the earth?"

"No, not at all. It's about time—"

"Well, then I don't understand," Margaret interrupted. "In the East the new wave is toward Native American spirituality. In Brattleboro, Vermont there is a really great shop that offers Indian artifacts—"

"More like artifakes," Rachel cut in drily. "Probably white-owned."

Margaret gave her a sour look, reluctantly admitting, "Well, yes, it might be, but they carry things from all over the country. A woman works there who makes personal prayer bags. She made mine. First she determines your totem animals from a deck of cards, then there is a short guided meditation and the rest of the items are added. For me it was a seashell, a piece of bone, and a twist of hair from my horse's tail."

"How much did this set you back?" Rachel asked.

Margaret looked offended.

"Why do you mind my asking?" Rachel released her hair clip and ran her fingers through the tangles in her hair as she watched Margaret.

"I don't see that that has anything to do with it."

"It has everything to do with it."

"One hundred and thirty-five dollars. That included the reading and contact with my animal guides, too." Margaret hurried on because Rachel's face told her that she was going to be challenged. "Yes, she was white, but she studied with an Indian teacher, well, mostly Indian, from South Dakota. Look, I'm not quite sure what you're driving at, but doesn't the market help keep the Indian spirituality alive?"

In a quiet, steady voice Rachel asked, "Don't you think they can do that without us?"

Still defensive, although just beginning to see there might be a point here that she was missing, Margaret said, "Well, I think it's wonderful that whites are looking to Native Americans for spiritual leadership."

Rachel loved Margaret, but she knew they might not agree on this issue. It was important to her to say what she had learned as clearly as possible. She began carefully, slowly choosing her words.

"It's true, we have a lot to learn from Native Americans. All of the wonderfully divergent tribes of them. But we tend to lump them all together—take this from the Crow, this from the Lakota, a bit here from the Arapaho, a little Hopi for spice. We call it all Indian. We trivialize. We define. We put their culture in the past tense and ignore the present, the ways we try to absorb and assimilate, the missionaries—yes, still at work—the Indian boarding schools. Kate's grandmother was forced to go to the government boarding school for Indians. Her father hid her in the mountains, did everything he could to keep her home and away from the indoctrination of the whites. It still goes on, though. The children are required to go to school, school is too far away to come home at night, so the children are forced to be separated from their homes and family culture. It's another more subtle form of Custer."

Rachel had to stop speaking for a moment; she knew her anger was overflowing. She kept her eyes on something neutral, the rug, the lamp, as she braided her hair for the night.

"We ignore the alcoholism, the high rate of suicide in children, the economic despair, as we walk into a shop, owned by whites, to buy 'Indian' artifacts mass-produced by whites. Totems and drums. Turkey feathers with a bit of rawhide and beads sold as "red hawk feather, use for sweeping your meditation site." It's insulting because it trivializes and commercializes what whites have never been able to respect. . .and we don't show our respect by walking into those stores and buying that stuff."

"Sit here beside me, please, I need to reconnect a little." Margaret reached out a hand to Rachel, who came to sit next to her in the orange plastic motel chair with a strip of duct tape on it. "This is pretty different thinking to absorb suddenly," Margaret admitted. "Here I was going along believing I was being honoring and respectful, and you tell me I haven't been."

Rachel sat quietly, her dark eyebrows lifted slightly. She only nodded her head once.

"It's hard to take that in, even though I have to admit what you are saying makes sense. But I know I'm not willing to give up my spiritual sense of connection to the earth that Native Americans have taught me."

"No need to," Rachel responded. "What we need to do is get clearer in our heads about where money comes into spirituality. I don't think it belongs there at all. I guess it's easy to become lazy or greedy in our search and as a result leave victims behind us."

Margaret lay down on her stomach across the bed and put her hand on Rachel's blue-jeaned knee. "Then you believe, and Kate too, that all these Indian artifakes, as you call them," she gave a little laugh, "are disrespectful copies made by whites ignorant of the depth of the culture they came from?"

A firm yes was the response.

"What about the animal guides workshops and spiritual tracking retreats?" Margaret asked, adding, "are you saying those are like the artifakes?"

Nodding, Rachel said, "If you look at the people leading those workshops I think you will find they are all white or claim a fuzzy Native American heritage. And if you ask Native Americans what they think of it all, you will hear disapproval."

Margaret took her own hair down now and rolled over on her back to stare at the stucco ceiling. "Wow," she said thoughtfully.

"What you say really does make enormous sense. I'm going to have to work on finding out where my views are in all this. Did you learn this from Kate?" Her eyes moved to question Rachel's eyes, upside down, as Rachel stood, then folded back the sheets.

"You know, I guess I did." Rachel's rough hand smoothed the white triangle, then softly rasped Margaret's cheek. "You and I got through that, didn't we? It was kind of scary, but not too bad." Her eyes crinkled at the corners. "Mind if I shower first?"

"No, go ahead," Margaret said as she rolled off the bed. She dug into her pack for her robe and hairbrush. As she brushed her hair she thought over their discussion. Margaret liked to be challenged in her thinking, although she certainly would fight for her opinions. She found her respect for Rachel deepening.

Twelve

K estrel pushed her whiskery muzzle into Rachel's hand as she undid the snap on the trailer tie. "This is it, girl," Rachel murmured. "Back. Easy now." Kestrel backed off the trailer, flung her mane, and pranced to the end of the leadline, her nostrils flared. Her tail flagged in a high arch like a rising wave.

After leading Kestrel around to limber up and see her surroundings, Rachel put her in a stall. She had been lucky to get one at the Squaw Valley stables, the staging area this year for the start of the ride. The mare settled, Rachel went off to find out what their place was and to register.

Margaret watched Rachel thread her way past the jockeying new arrivals, her body supple and confident. Margaret's own body was swept with a tingling sweetness that circled her pelvis and centered in a warmth that ebbed out her knees. Kate's slow chuckle brought her back. "You two. A scandal to the jaybirds."

Margaret turned and smiled at Kate. "She is lovely to look at."

"And, no doubt, delightful to hold, but we've got work to do," Kate said as she unloaded the wheelbarrow and shovel from the storage half of the horse trailer. She cleaned and swept out the manure while Margaret finished unloading the grain, hay, and buckets. They both carried the heavy tack trunk over to rest beside the stall. All the things Rachel would need to get the mare ready for the vetting were laid out on the railing by the stall.

Both stood, independently going over their mental checklists, side by side but on different thought islands. Margaret breathed deeply, her list completed. She turned to Kate to say,

"I want to thank you for not staying silent last night. I would like to talk with you more about it. Rachel was very helpful, and got me over the hurdle of my initial confusion. I'm glad she could do that. You shouldn't have to deal with whites' righteous indignation." She laughed a little, embarrassed.

Kate's smile was broad as she retied her red bandanna. "I had some faith in you. I went through a few ugly scenes, though, with people I thought were my friends. Turned out they weren't friends but Indian lovers, and what I was saying didn't fit their picture."

Kate walked out to where she could see the full expanse of the Squaw Valley complex, then turned to Margaret. "This place. It's named the white word that is universally derogatory to Native American women, but no one even hears it. It's like naming Dr. Martin Luther King Day "Nigger Day." I wouldn't mind if there was a nationwide petition to change the name." She grinned at Margaret. "In the meantime, I guess we should finish up around here. I'm going to move the rig over to the parking area."

Kate opened the truck door and then froze at the sight of Rachel, walking back. She was a changed woman. "What the hell," Kate muttered. She softly closed the truck door.

Margaret had seen her too. They both moved forward. Rachel waved them back. She had a combatant's look about her, but it was fragile—there to keep back the tears. She wiped her hand across her face, eyes fierce between her fingers.

"It's off. I can't ride." She had to stop and swallow. She looked at Kestrel, who was watching her over the stall door, then rapidly away.

"Why?" Margaret cried.

"It has something to do with the Forest Service limiting the number of horses on the trail. The ride committee has been overbooking this ride by fifty horses every year in order to take care of the no-shows. But they haven't kept up with the fact that over the last thirty years people have learned a lot about conditioning their horses and keeping them fit. This year they didn't get away with it. They have thirty more horses than they can let start. The vets are being ruthless on the initial vetting to dump off entries, but the manager just told me that the last entries accepted will be bumped. I'm one of the last."

While passing on this information, Rachel had maintained a detached steel-like tone, but at the end her voice caught in a groan. She turned away from the women, who were still trying to accept the situation as real, to pace a small circle. She could not quite bring herself to load up and head back to Montana.

A lanky young man walked up to them as Rachel was talking. "Excuse me," he said in a beautiful voice with a Southwest rhythm. "I guess you are in a bad place right now, but I had an idea. I was in the office and overheard what the manager said to you. It sure seems like a raw deal. I heard you and your horse came a long way for this ride and that you are among the frontrunners. Look, I'm just in it for a lark. Why don't you take my place?"

Nobody could believe their ears. *Who was this guy?* Rachel pulled herself together to answer. "That's very nice of you, but I can't do that Mr. . . ."

"Garcia. Garcia Mendez." They shook hands. "Hey, if I am very lucky, I might be able to complete the ride in twenty-four hours and never walk again." He laughed. "I planned to pull out at Robinson Flat or, at best, Michigan Bluff." He looked over at Kestrel, admiring her. "Now that horse has the look of a winner." He smiled at Rachel. "You do, too. Let's go see about making an exchange."

Rachel stood rooted, afraid to accept, trying to sense if there were any sexual overtones. "But you don't even know me. What could I ever do to repay you?" she asked, her wary feelers fully extended.

"I don't expect anything in return. I don't even know why I'm doing it, except that it seems the right thing." His lean face was friendly and kind.

Rachel's body relaxed as she realized that Garcia was simply doing what he thought was right. "I know you've worked hard to get here too, so I want you to know that I really appreciate your offer." She grinned. "And I'm going to take you up on it."

The collective sigh from behind her made Rachel turn around. Margaret and Kate were hugging each other in relief.

After much thanking of Garcia, all four trooped off to the small ski chalet serving as the Western States Trail Ride office. They were not the only group with ruffled feathers. There seemed more than a few bumped contestants who wouldn't fold their tents, load their horses, and drive meekly away. Eventually, space was gained just in front of the ride manager's desk, and Garcia presented his proposal.

"Are you a relative of Ms. Duncan?" the ride manager asked.

"What's that got to do with it?" Garcia responded.

"Only relatives can take a withdrawing rider's place. Otherwise, the place is sold to the next person on the waiting list." His eyes nervously scanned the people still waiting to air their complaints.

"That's a stupid rule," Rachel stated firmly. "Where does it say that?"

Sighing, the ride manager shuffled through papers until he dug out a copy of the letter sent to all entrants. "Here," he said, handing it to her. "It is a rule."

"It's an unfair one. How many families have more than one horse or rider capable of the Tevis Cup? Not many." Rachel's indignation was in full swing. "And it's very unfair to singles. It's one of those family-centered rules that get my goat."

The mellow voice of Garcia gently intervened. "How many riders are ahead of her?"

"Twenty-three," the ride manager said, glancing at a clipboard on the desk. "We have thirty more entries than we should have here. Almost all of the horses are passing their initial vetting, and a higher percentage than normal have kept sound since they entered. We expected a much higher attrition rate." He smiled. "Speaks well of the sport, don't you think?"

Rachel snorted and stomped out. She agreed with him, but she sure wasn't into being agreeable. It was clear to her that he was just a harried official squeezed between the policies of the Tevis Cup Committee and the National Forest Service.

Garcia followed her out and found her relating the story to Margaret and Kate, standing on the dry-packed earth in front of the chalet. When Garcia joined them, Margaret said, "Nice try." Kate nodded her agreement.

"Thanks, Garcia," Rachel managed to get out. She was making an enormous effort to hold herself together, the devastating disappointment quickly washing in on the ebbing tide of anger.

"Yeah." He squinted up at the sun, edging past noon, and said, "Too bad it didn't work, though. If you come up with another idea, the offer still stands. Nice meet'n you all." He lifted his hat just clear of his head, a gentleman cowboy of another era.

Rachel's steps quickened as she walked back to her horse. Her friends let her go, knowing she needed to be away from people and near the silent comfort of her mare. Margaret and Kate walked slowly, allowing the bleak reality to sink in.

They found Rachel sitting in the dark corner of the stall, Kestrel's soft breath moving the stray wisps of hair on the top of her head. She rose to her feet, slid her hand down along Kestrel's neck, ending in a pat, then came out the stall door. Moving in a fog of disappointment, she gathered the buckets, put them in the truck, opened the tack trunk lid, took out the shipping boots, then stood, staring blankly into the trunk.

Margaret closed the trunk lid, then sat on it. "Let's take this slow."

"What's there to take?" Rachel responded, lips firm, face stony.

"Rachel, what is most important to you—the personal test of doing the ride or the completion buckle. . .or even the cup?"

Rachel's expression changed from granite to curiosity. What was this woman driving at? "That's easy. Just knowing we can do it is what's most important." She took a long look at Margaret. Kate let in a quick breath of air. "Are you saying I should just do it without being entered?"

"That's exactly what I'm saying."

"You know I couldn't do that, Margaret." She picked up the grooming things all nicely laid out for her to use, dumped them into the carrying kit, then threw it all into the back of the pickup: brushes, hook pick, everything, bouncing off the truck cap, scattering among the sleeping and duffel bags. "Damn," she said in the settling dust, "I can't just ignore the Forest Service's effort to regulate the wear and tear on the trail because I want to do the ride. I mean, I agree with their ruling."

"You mean you wouldn't be number 251?" Margaret asked.

"No. It would be a terrible precedent. If I finished well, there might be some publicity about it. Everybody loves a renegade. Next thing you know every fool in the country would be down here ignoring the rules. The Forest Service would damn sure close the trail access if that happened."

Margaret stood watching her, listening to her, loving her strong values and stubbornness in upholding them. "Hold on a minute," she said, moving over to Rachel and gently taking the water bucket out of her hand. "Let's sit over here in the shade. I have a proposition, and if you don't like it, we'll pack up. O.K.?"

When they were all three seated on the soft pine needles, Margaret continued. "If Garcia is serious about his offer, and I think he is, then he could start with the rest, rendezvous with you up the trail about a mile, then drop out. You still wouldn't be a legal entry, but you could do the ride and there would be no additional horses on the trail. You would be an entry if that rule about family-only transfer were changed." Margaret raised her eyebrows at Rachel. "What do you think?"

Rachel was very thoughtful. "I believe he would, but that's just the beginning hurdle crossed. It would never work. I could never complete the ride without the support of the ride volunteers." Shaking her head, she was skeptical even in the face of the two eager women sitting opposite her.

"Kate and I could set up your water stops," Margaret said, her eyes briefly catching Kate's to check that this was so.

Nodding, Kate said, "You don't have to use any of the management's facilities."

"I can vet you through the checkpoints," Margaret said, "although you may need to brief me on what to look for. If we put the number zero on Kestrel's hip, everyone will know you're not a formal entry. And we can do it all by the rules, so you'll know how well you did."

A change came into Rachel's eyes. She was starting to hope. She was also afraid of hoping. Already today her spirits had soared and dropped so many times she felt like an aging steeplechaser.

"Some of the areas are really remote, with no roads. How would you get in there?" She asked the question, but Margaret could see she was willing to take on the challenge.

"We'll ask around," Kate said. "Let's at least find out if it's possible."

"As your crew, that will be our job. Your job is to ride that trail," added Margaret.

Kate strode off to "explore the possibilities," as she put it. She came back a very short time later, urging on, like a sheepdog, a wizened, white-haired woman. "This is Mollie. She's a mule packer and knows these parts."

Mollie's brown eyes were intelligent, sharp, and assessing, surrounded by a face latticed with a fine cobweb of wrinkles. Her dusky voice came out soft and strong. "This gal tells me you want to do the ride on your own. I think you must be crazy, but that kind of crazy I've always gone in for." She chuckled. "I'll help you if I can."

Rachel and Margaret stared a little longer than was polite at the old woman in her patched blue jeans and ratty sheepskin vest. Margaret took over. "We need to get water and food to drop-off points that Rachel can easily find. We need someone who knows the territory and can get them there. And we need help planning the logistics of our support."

"I can do that. Hold on a minute." Mollie turned and faded off through the jumble of trailers toward the parking lot. The three of them watched her retreating aged back.

"Do you think she can?" Rachel breathed softly.

"I hope she's not cracked or senile," Margaret said. She paused, considering, "Yes, I think she can."

Kate, used to her grandmother's strong old women friends, said matter-of-factly, "She's old enough to know what she can do."

"By morning we'll know if the support is in place. If I'm not absolutely satisfied you and Kestrel will have what you need, we'll scrub it." Margaret turned to Kate. "I have a sneaking feeling we're going to be up all night. Do you think you can do that and still function as crew tomorrow?"

"You bet. It really matters to me to see them cross the finish line."

Mollie hove into view with greasy battered maps waving beside her like bat wings. She kicked aside a pile of horse manure, knelt on the ground, and spread them out, arranging the torn pieces so they matched. "Oh, Rachel," she said, "I ran into some old coot in the parking lot claims she's a pal of yours." Mollie's *heh heh heh* settled down around her shoulders as she hunched over the map.

"Who?"

The eager brown eyes that looked back up at Rachel told her she was just waiting to be asked. "June. Said she would crew up with us. Flew here in that damn contraption of hers. Maybe we can put it to some use. Hmm."

Mollie shoved her knuckles under her nose and rested her whole face on them, studying the map. Then she licked her thumb and used it to smooth and groom her bushy eyebrows. Very catlike, Margaret thought, just as Mollie hawked and spat, ruining the feline effect.

"Now, as I see it," Mollie said, taking charge again, "your mare will need water every ten miles. Five when it gets hot." She received a confirming nod from Rachel. "It's about sixteen miles from Squaw Valley to the American River. No water on the way and a nine-thousand-foot pass between. What do you want to do about that?" she asked drily.

"That's one of the places I've been thinking about," Rachel answered. "Seems to me a lot of riders burn their horses up right at the start. I'd like to take that pass fairly slow and somewhere before we hit Red Star Ridge, where we can stretch out, I'd like to stoke up Kestrel. Replace some of the energy she used getting over that mountain. I want to start out light—the bare minimum of 165 pounds you have to have to win the Tevis." Her voice choked off. Coughing to clear it, but noticed by Mollie, she went on. "Everything—me, my clothes, the saddle, bridle, and pack—165. I don't want to carry anything extra over that mountain. So around here," she pointed to an area just before Red Star Ridge, "I want a stash of water and a bit of hay and grain for Kestrel and some water and food for me."

Molly was studying Rachel pretty closely. "We can do that," she said. "From there on, you won't have any trouble finding water for your mare. We can give you a map with the good watering places marked. The main problem is water for you." She pointed at the thirty-odd miles that lay past Robinson Flat's one-hour hold. "This stretch is all rough canyon land. By the time you get there it'll feel like Hades. The canyon roads are restricted access this year to riders' crews."

"I will need to get in there somehow," Margaret said. "Even though she will be carrying her own stethoscope from Robinson Flat on, she will need a double check and also a little refueling. Where do you think we can do it, Mollie?"

Mollie lifted her hat and scratched the already scrambled hair. Reverting to her mule-packer voice, she said, "Yup, that piece of property lives up to its names—Devil's Thumb, Last Chance. The Deadwood Road is closed off too. Christ. Last year you should have seen it. Two hundred-fifty four-wheel-drive vehicles, half with horse trailers hitched, tearing around these roads. The dust was enough to close off the sun, couldn't see a damn thing for hundreds of yards. I sat up on Cuckoo Ridge and watched the show. Nobody could get where they needed to be. It was a mess." She chuckled, the fondly remembered day shining out of her memory.

Rocking back on her heels, she finally got around to answering Margaret's question. "Oh, we'll get in there somehow or other. Might take some thought." Mollie scuffled her body into a more comfortable position. "From Michigan Bluff to Foresthill is a little less than fifteen miles. We can meet you there with the truck. Then another twenty to Francisco's—vehicles are off-limits there, too. About twelve miles to the crossing at Highway 49, then only six miles or less to Auburn."

June sauntered up to the coven huddle. "Hi, Tiger." She lifted Mollie's hat to ruffle her hair, then winked at the others.

"You flying reprobate, leave my hair alone." Settling her hat deeper, Mollie tried to use the brim to cover her blush and shy, pleased smile.

"So you two have already been introduced?" Rachel observed.

"Might put it that way," June said drily. "How's the strategy coming?"

Mollie said, "One of the hitches is that crew access is severely limited and the crews are encouraged to carpool. It will be hard to get a ride with the others. Impossible with all the gear we need at the one-hour holds. There's no way around it. The gear will have to be hauled in tonight, so it will free you up tomorrow, Margaret, to get a ride with somebody. Robinson Flat is the farthest. Maybe we can drop off supplies there after we've packed the mules in to the Red Star Ridge spot."

Rachel ran her finger along the canyon section that worried them. "This part here, June, is a stinker."

June studied the map and found what she was looking for. "Look here, Mollie. There's a small airport at Cedar Springs. Could you get the mules down here to take one of us cross-country to this spring here, just past Last Chance?"

Kate burst out, "Hey, that's great."

They all looked at Mollie, whose enthusiasm was much less pronounced as she slowly traced her finger along the miles of switchback dirt roads, calculating the hours it would take to haul the gooseneck rig loaded with three mules. She looked up at Rachel. "If you are riding at your best speed, when do you figure on reaching this area?"

Rachel took her time answering, figuring in the terrain, the heat, her pacing. "I don't expect to hit this spot before noon. After Michigan Bluff we can make some time."

"I can get the mules there, but there is no way to get Margaret there and back in time for the check and hour's hold at Michigan Bluff. It's going to have to be you, June, who makes the check. It's at least an hour's trek in to this point."

"O.K., I'll do it. Then I can fly out to the airport at Foresthill and meet the gang there."

"It's going to take me a while coming out over Mosquito Ridge," Molly said.

Rachel suddenly felt exhausted standing on the edge of this intense planning group. I've got to turn this all over to them, she thought. *Now that June is in on the crew, they have an experienced distance rider who can answer any questions. They don't need me. Margaret is right, my job is to do the ride and trust them to do the rest.* She studied them in turn, one at a time, no longer hearing what they said, and knew that each of these strong women brought special qualities that made them an effective whole. She felt her energy return. Stepping back, she said, "I'm going to take a walk."

She snapped a lead on Kestrel's halter, and the two of them went as far away from people as they could get. Far up on a ski slope, they found some grass. Kestrel's slow methodical grazing restored them both. Rachel had discovered a side run of the slope with a safe quiet ring of trees between them and the charged energy in the valley.

"I will promise you right now, sweet friend, that I will listen to what you tell me. If you are tired, we rest; hungry, we eat; had enough of this game, we will simply go home. Your long life, fitness, and happiness mean the most to me. So there."

Kestrel stopped grazing to raise her head, listening, dark eyes intent and ears studiously still. When Rachel had finished, hands on hips, eye contact held for the time of a bird's flight across the sky, Kestrel sighed, started chewing again, then lowered her head to the grass, relaxed and unwary.

Thirteen

A complaining growl reminded Rachel that her stomach was neglected. Slowly she eased herself back into civilization, feeling much more calm.

She found June and Margaret in the stable area, still working out complicated plans that Rachel purposefully sent past her own ears, up and over her head to catch a breeze. It was about five o'clock. Kate and Mollie had left an hour before, they told her. "We're going out to dinner, then we'll drop you off at the motel," Margaret said briskly, still in her "planning voice."

Rachel, looking up from gathering together Kestrel's dinner, responded, "That'll sit right with me."

Caught strongly by Rachel's nonchalant butchness, Margaret leaned close and whispered, "My cowgirl."

Rachel just raised one eyebrow and shook her head as June headed for the facilities. "A dusty cowgirl," she said. The west corner of her mouth lifted as she swept the top of each worn brown boot across the back of each calf, then slapped and brushed at her blue jeans. When she undid her belt to tuck in her shirt, Margaret felt a rush of desire.

"So where is this joint?" Rachel asked, unaware of Margaret's altered state.

Gathering herself together, Margaret answered, "It's overlooking Lake Tahoe. The food is supposed to be as good as the view."

Rachel admired her golden woman in the late afternoon light. "If you are my view, I could eat at a greasy spoon." She took a step toward Margaret who, seeing June returning, gave a slight shake of her head. Rachel backed off with a blush, then with a flash of anger kicked the straw at her feet.

June strode up with a knowing look on her face. "Oh, relax, you two. Why do you think I cleared out? I thought you might like some time alone. I already figured out about your special friendship. Mollie and I have been pretty tight for years, too. 'Long about thirty, I'd say." She patted Rachel with big whamming pats, the sort horse people invariably give both their horses and each other. "If the truth be known, that's why I got that fool plane and learned to fly it. Mollie can't bear to live with anyone. Needs to be alone most of the time. I don't know what I'll do when I get too old to fly. Move into her barn, maybe. If I wiggle my ears and bray, she may let me stay near her."

Laughing, they got into the truck, then drove to where June had left her rented Camaro. Rachel felt a tremendous relief to be open around June, whom she had known and liked for years. It was affirming to her and her love of Margaret that another woman she respected also loved a woman. The amount of sheer space around each person in the mountain West guaranteed an individuality, a singularity; however, overseeing all was an unyielding sheeplike conservatism that worked to keep everyone in line with the threat of further isolation. While the community attitudes about lesbians were almost never expressed—the community apparently agreeing with Queen Victoria that women wouldn't do such things—she had heard lots of insulting fag warnings to guys who didn't cram themselves into the macho mold. The struggle for Rachel had been basic: overcoming her negative feelings about women. In some ways, being able to allow herself to love Margaret was the sign that she had come to a place of respect and affection with herself.

The food and view at the Tahoe Belle were great. It was just after 6:30 when they left a generous tip and paid the dinner bill. On their way out, Rachel was greeted by a number of other riders, offering her drinks. She shook her head as she walked to the car park, saying, "I don't know how they do it. Half those riders and their crews will be up till late, drinking and all." Aware of how prudish she sounded, she added, "Well, you two will be up all night, so how can I talk?" She stopped suddenly. "Are you sure you want to be doing all this?"

"It's a little late to worry about that with Mollie and Kate careening around the old stomping ground of the Donner party at this very moment," June replied.

Rachel grinned her most sheepish grin. "You've got a point."

Back at Squaw Valley, Rachel fed Kestrel her evening hay, then measured out her morning feed. Margaret would drive the truck hauling the gear-laden horse trailer. Earlier that day Mollie and Margaret had sorted the mass of feed and gear into two piles: the stuff needed by June and Margaret went into the trailer; the rest was jammed into Mollie's ancient truck she called the Tin Lezzie.

"It's like me," Mollie had said. "You think it won't start each morning, then damned if it don't."

The dog-eared Piney Peek Motel, a strong contrast to the Best Western up the road in Truckee, had cottages with tiny kitchens. Best of all, though, they were far from each other, being billed as honeymoon cottages. Rachel and Margaret drove to the one farthest from the highway.

The front porch with its solitary rocker was covered with a velvety throw of pine needles. Rachel pushed some off the boards with her boot, commenting, "Looks like they could stand a little more traffic around here." She let herself in with the key dangling from the large maroon tag, No. 7, and eyed the bed that took more than half the room. It was already 7:15, and she needed to be asleep by eight if she could manage it. She threw her bag on the only chair and worried about getting to sleep. It had been a rip-roaring, emotionally packed day. Margaret came in with her saddle and a tape player. "I brought one of my meditation tapes. This one is the ocean. Maybe it will help you get to sleep."

"Thank you. I was just wondering how I'd do that. I won't use sleeping pills and I've never tried tapes before. . . ." She trailed off, aware that soon she would be alone here. "What I would really like is your soothing body next to mine."

Margaret came to her, arms gently enfolding. "Been a rough day, hasn't it, love?"

"Yes. And it'll be a rough night for you and June. When do you think you'll be done?"

"I'm not sure. June will fly to Foresthill to meet me and the truck and trailer. After we set up everything, we'll leave the rig there and fly back. I will definitely be back by three to feed Kestrel, then come to wake you." Margaret gave her a quick kiss, then set up the tape recorder and put the tape in the slot.

Laughing somewhat nervously, Rachel said, "This isn't going to make me want to join an ashram, is it? You know, subliminal advertising or something?"

Margaret let out a burst of laughter, took a step back, and shook her head. "Am I quietly meditating in an ashram? No, I'm here in California, abetting a mad woman. I can assure you I've listened to this tape many times and all that's on it is a recording of the ocean. I think you will be safe from any influence."

She rolled her eyes as Rachel crept up on her in a stalking sneak attack, taking Margaret's belt flap in her teeth, growlingly shaking it, and mumbling out from between her teeth, "You are not safe from your influence on me."

Taking her wild one by the elbows, Margaret lifted her to her lips. She kissed her, then said, "Good night, *femme sauvage*."

A little later, after a deliciously long hot shower, Rachel opened all the windows so the gauzy curtains could lift and fall with the slight breeze, pushed the Play button on the tape machine, and slid into the cool sheets. The slow rise and fall of the waves echoed the curtains, bringing her breathing into harmony without her awareness. The small suck after each wave pulled with it thousands of tiny pebbles, their clink of touching reminiscent of wind chimes. An untamed sound. She was asleep well before the soft click at the end of the tape.

Fourteen

As Margaret took the west ramp for Interstate 80, she noticed the scenic route signs for Donner Pass. Mollie and Kate would be traveling the same area the Donner party were lost in over a hundred years ago.

She smiled as she remembered cramming all the stuff for Robinson Flat and Red Star Ridge into the back of Mollie's Tin Lezzie. It had taken about an hour to sort the gear into the two trucks and the horse trailer. Margaret hoped she would have energy left after the long night ahead, not only to be functional during the race but also to be enthusiastically present for Rachel. She settled in for the long drive to Auburn.

Mollie drove south along the western rim of Lake Tahoe. Just past Meeks Bay she angled west. Her pack station was nicely placed on the edge of both the El Dorado National Forest and the Desolation Valley Primitive Area.

Mollie's small ranch was almost hidden by a grove of aspens that led up the mountain from Lake Jenifer in a long curling wisp. A herd of about twenty pretty little mules grazed in the meadow. They raised their heads in unison to watch Mollie swing open the gate to the corral. At her whistle they trotted single-file in their order of dominance, without fuss, into the corral. They were a mix of bays and greys, most standing barely under the maximum pony height, 14.2 hands. One, with a black dorsal stripe and a cross over the shoulders, snuffled into Kate's pockets.

"Here now, Friar, get your nose out of there." Mollie pushed the friendly mule away. "I give them too many handouts. Turned them into little beggars."

Kate grinned. "They're all so pretty and friendly, it would be hard to say no to them."

Pride glowed in Mollie's eyes. "I had never been around Arab horses much until June talked me into helping on the Tevis Cup ride one year. I can tell you, I was impressed at how tough those pretty Arabs are. Seeing that changed my breeding ideas. I bought a few Arab mares cheap. Not show quality." She made a snooty face, then winked at Kate. "I breed those mares to the best donkey stallions I can find. Every year I sell one or two. Packers around here have finally wised up. These are hardy, tough little suckers and as sweet and willing as you please. They are smaller than the mules I used to have, but I tell you, they go farther with the same size load in better humor."

"I don't know anything about mules," Kate said.

"You will learn. If you'll catch up these three"—Mollie pointed them out—"I'll hitch the rig and fill the water tanks. Halters and lead ropes are just inside the barn door." She scuttled off.

Within a sharp thirty minutes they were loaded, the old steel gooseneck trailer rattling and banging down the rough dirt road like a rolling junkyard. The deafening clatter dramatically let up when the rig reached the paved road. Shifting up to third gear, Mollie said, "There's a good thirty-five miles of smooth road ahead. Gives us a chance to get some talking done before we hit the back roads."

With relief, Kate retied her bandanna shaken loose by the jolting corduroyed road, as well as the truck's failed suspension.

"How do you feel about climbing on a mule?" Mollie asked with a quick darting glance.

"Sure will be a first," Kate allowed. "So far I haven't seen any sign of their bad reputation. You know, it bothers me the stereotypes different breeds of horses have."

Mollie agreed. "I always believed what people said about Arabians. You know, too delicate, flighty space cases, all that. Now I laugh when people call them living works of art. I heard that once down in Scottsdale. I can tell you, I laughed fit to piss my pants."

Kate laughed, but soon her face became serious. "People do the same thing to each other, don't they? When I had to leave my family to board out so I could go to the regional high school, I became an *Indian*. Some were openly hostile; others idealized everything Indian. They both tried to fit me into their picture of who I was. It was a relief to go home vacations and be Kate Singer—horsewoman, poet, crossword puzzle expert, Lakota, piano player, and sister, granddaughter, child." She pulled the visor down to block some of the setting sun, then sat crosswise to see Mollie. Funny, she thought, the way passengers sit staring fixedly ahead through the windshield, as if they don't trust the driver to keep an eye on the road.

Mollie stuffed some loose white hairs back under her hat. Her eyebrows, with wild, stray cat-whisker hairs, lowered. "People call mules stubborn. Seems to me humans are slower to learn and harder to shift out of a comfortable place." Her eyes were serious as she glanced at Kate.

Time and miles passed as they exchanged stories and training methods, enjoying each other's company.

Mollie eyed the sun as she slowed for the turnoff at Soda Springs. The last words Kate heard for the next thirty minutes were, "I'd like to make it up the canyon before dark."

The road reached south in a series of switchbacks—up ridges, down to creeks. At the place called the Cedars, they pulled off to the left to follow the river upstream. Kate saw a Forest Service sign there, pointing out the Pacific Crest Trail 3.6 miles and Painted Rock 1.2 miles.

They parked at Painted Rock. As the silence rushed in to fill the vacuum after the deafening roar from the stock trailer, Kate felt it almost as a physical change. Finally, when the small sounds of birds, the water rushing by, and the trailer ramp being lowered could reach her ears in their delicacy, she moved to help unload the mules.

Painted Rock took the evening light into itself, then seemed to radiate the colors as if lit from within. The heat of the day, now just an echo of what it had been, was still intense enough to raise a gleam of sweat on the mules, darkening the bays to mahogany and the grey to slate.

While Kate saddled the riding mules—Friar and the grey, Chalk—Mollie placed the pack saddle and harness on Sherpa. Standing on either side of the mule, they lifted the lightweight panniers onto the crossbars. Made out of fiberglass, these had been designed by Mollie with a lower section that took five gallons of water on each side, filled with a hose or hand pump and emptied by a spigot. Above was a compartment to hold grain, closed by a canvas flap which left room on top for other gear. The panniers were shaped like kidney beans, so there were no corners to catch on rocks or trees. Mollie tied four buckets to the top of the load, spread a tarp over all, and then threw a diamond hitch over the load and tightened it down. Kate watched with admiration as Mollie made the notoriously complicated diamond look like jump rope, or some other kids' game.

She was still standing there, wondering how anyone could commit it to memory, when Mollie hit the saddle and started up the trail. Kate untied Friar, put her toe in the stirrup, and was halfway up when she remembered she hadn't tightened the cinch. Suddenly she was standing on the ground with her boot still in the stirrup, the saddle hanging under Friar's belly like a slipped girdle. She frantically tried to untangle herself before the mule freaked out and bolted across the countryside, dragging her over the rough terrain. Her near panic was interrupted by a long-suffering sigh. She looked up into Friar's very large patient eyes and said, "I'm sorry." Then she giggled. Once she had extricated her wedged foot from the stirrup, straightened and recinched the saddle, she was soon mounted and ready to ride. They found Mollie and the other mules a short way up the trail, where a creek joined the river.

"Trouble?" Mollie raised her eyebrows.

Kate flushed a crimson glow and mumbled, "Not much." To herself, the uncensored version was, *Damn silly greenhorn thing to do—not check the cinch.*

Mollie turned in the saddle, then urged Chalk up the creek's canyon. In the last of the day's dry heat, the quick click of mule shoes bounced off the canyon walls like castanets. Up ahead it looked to Kate as if the trail ended in a jumble of rock. Mollie swung down and unsnapped the lead rope from Sherpa, turning her loose. "We'll walk for a bit," she said.

"She won't run off?" Kate asked with a worried look.

"Nah, they do better on their own," Mollie explained before she disappeared up a narrow crack running the face of what looked to be a sheer wall.

Kate scrambled after, trying to get her feet to follow the hind feet of Friar. The slanting light accented the shadows on the rock and played tricks with depth perception. After about fifty feet of sharp rise, she was reminded of the time she had tried rock climbing in Yosemite. She'd had a rope then. She wished she hadn't remembered; her stomach and the sun both had that sinking feeling. She stopped for breath once, only to become aware that Friar was patiently perched on a ledge that was virtually invisible.

A brick-red shape, like a piece of the setting sun, swooped by very close to her right shoulder. Another. Bats. In age-old fear Kate crouched and covered her head as Friar carefully stepped on up the trail and out of sight. The pair skimmed by again, nearly sending her over the edge into a scream. *Can't*, she told herself firmly. *If I scream, Mollie will for sure think I'm a wimp. After all, these are just little flying rodents that eat bugs.* That left her out. Even though at present, she felt a little crawly.

Kate tried to adopt a naturalist's viewpoint on the entire drama. *Red bats. Hmm, very interesting.* It helped that the bats chose that moment to fly off to their hunting grounds. She scrambled on up after Friar. In the last remnants of light, she rounded a boulder to find Friar with his pals and Mollie lounging under a stunted pine on what passed right then for level ground.

Kate collapsed beside Mollie and had a few words to say about the climb up the so-called trail. "Rachel won't be very happy with you if her wrangler gets killed on this venture," she ended.

"Now you been up in broad daylight, it'll be a snap coming back later," Mollie drawled, watching for a reaction.

She got it. All the color drained from Kate's face. She asked, "In the dark?" Then sat up, squared her shoulders, and said, "I won't do it. There must be another way to go." Enough of the light had dimmed that she no longer could see Mollie's face, but she heard the chuckle. "Very funny. Did you bring me along just for a laugh?"

Mollie rose to her feet and was quiet for a minute. When she spoke again, her voice was sober. "Sorry. I know you were scared. I also know you've got a lot of grit. The guys do that kind of teasing all the time, and I got used to it, but it's not kind. I guess they tend to think like it's some kind of test they are on when they are together in the wilds."

They were both quiet then. Kate, still sitting, could see Mollie only as a hard-edged silhouette, the upper half of her a dark velvet plum color. Her hands hanging at her side were outlined in a fierce raspberry, with orange coming up the slit between her legs and back-lighting the wrinkles in her jeans. Her eyes moved over to the ridge that they were headed for, where the dark reds bled into the rocks and sent up sharp fir trees to roughen the sky.

Mollie pointed off to the southwest. "We are aiming just to the right of Mount Mildred, which is just about due south. See that bit of rock outcrop? That's where we pick up the trail."

Kate scanned the flickering rim of the world. Far off was a sharp spine with a crisp wildness. She heard Mollie say, "That's Cougar Rock. Tomorrow it will be bristling with lurking shutterbugs."

Kate smiled. It was true. Every photograph she had seen of Tevis Cup participants had been taken as they came up over Cougar Rock. It was rugged, but only fifteen miles into the ride so the horses all still looked alert and fresh. Suitable for framing. Not as they would look by Devil's Thumb or Last Chance.

Chalk pawed the ground and shook his head, jingling the bridle. "Well, we came this way to save time," Mollie said. "Best not waste it." She dug into her saddlebags and pulled out two carbide lamps on head loops. Handing one to Kate, she explained how they worked. "These are better than flashlights because they light where you're going and leave your hands free. Miners' lights."

While Kate was still fiddling with the flint lighting device on the carbide lamp she could see Chalk's white rump disappear off through the dusk. Friar jiggled and fretted until Kate finally gave in and said, "O.K., for cry'n out loud, go ahead." With great relief at not being left to the tigers and lions, Friar shot forward, nearly unseating his rider.

A horrifying but luckily brief ride followed, with Friar careening down an invisible path and Kate desperately trying to light the unfamiliar light. It suddenly and bright as day came to her that it was she, and not the mule, who needed the light.

It was a snap then, of course. It also did not hurt matters that Friar caught up with his buddy, and Chalk's slightly hunched rider, now clearly illuminated.

Mollie turned off the trail at a cluster of piñon trees. She swung down from Chalk, spat into a creosote bush, then reached into her saddlebag to bring out a portable fluorescent light.

"Better turn off the carbides 'til we are done around here." She pulled a compass from her pocket and walked around, grunting occasionally, absorbed in her figuring.

"What are you doing?" Kate finally had to ask.

"Trying to figure where the sun will be tomorrow between seven and eight." She glanced up at Kate. "Supposed to be a scorcher. Let's keep them cool as long as we can. I think the other side of these two trees will give them the best shade." Mollie got the shovel out of its holster on the pack saddle, handed it to Kate, and said, "Dig over there," indicating a spot under the trees.

Kate walked over to the spot, stared blankly at it, raised her eyes to Mollie busily unpacking Sherpa, and asked, "What am I digging for? A latrine?"

Mollie stopped what she was doing and gazed across the mule's pack at Kate. It had never occurred to her that Kate wouldn't know why. "It's to keep the water cool. Holes to put the buckets in so they stay cool," she patiently explained, as if to someone deprived of a brain. She immediately commenced rummaging in the panniers again, pulling out sponge, gallon ziplock bag with grain, Rachel's food and water pack, a hay net, and dumping them untidily on the ground next to her. As she picked up the plastic buckets with snap lids, she glanced over at Kate burrowing away, saying, "Make it big enough for two."

For a while only the chunk of the shovel against sand and

rock could be heard as Mollie arranged the other details of the pit stop. From a low tree branch she hung a bucket with the bagged grain in it, then snapped on the lid. Next to it she hung a hay net with a small amount of alfalfa hay. Into a second bucket she emptied the contents of a zip-lock bag, then added about a quart of water, to make an electrolyte solution. Most everyone had their favorite recipe to replace the salts that were lost in sweat. At rider gatherings one could always overhear at least one hotly contested recipe—its miracle benefits, cost per dose, who had used it on which ride, and of course won. She dumped in a turkey baster so Rachel could squirt the solution into Kestrel's mouth, then snapped on the lid. Horse taken care of, Mollie then put in a small mesh bag Rachel's fixings: water bottle, apple, granola bar. She hung it in a tree by a cord with a quick-release knot.

"It's beginning to feel like Christmas, the way I'm decorating this tree," she drawled over her shoulder at Kate. "How's it going?"

"I think it's about done. Bring over your buckets and let's give it a try," Kate replied as she leveled the bottom.

Mollie set the buckets in the hole, pronounced it to be "mighty fine," and started pushing dirt and sand around the sides. When about four inches stood up above ground level, Mollie took the lids off, led Sherpa up, and attached a short hose to the spigot. After one bucket was filled, she turned the mule around to fill the second bucket from the other pannier, keeping Sherpa's load equal. One bucket for drinking, one to sponge over Kestrel to keep her cool. Mollie tossed a large sponge in one bucket, then snapped the lids on both.

Standing back to survey their newly created rest stop, Kate said, "Looks kind of homey."

"Don't it, though?" Mollie said, linking her arm in Kate's and wrinkling her eyes.

Kate felt close to Mollie then and realized she had been wary around this slightly fierce old woman. Suddenly she frowned. "How will Rachel know it's here?"

Mollie reached into her never-failing saddlebags and pulled out a roll of lavender surveyor's tape. Her big, roughly seamed hands got her pocketknife open and cut off a bunch of the delicate long streamers. "You ride up the trail about two hundred yards, hang one; then on the way back about a hundred yards, hang two. I'll put three here where she can see them from the trail."

Soon they were on their way back to the Cedars and the parked rig. Retracing their route only a short distance, Mollie cut off to the left on a clear trail that meandered around but eventually put them out on the Baker/Soda Springs road. Turning right brought them back after a while to the Cedars. Loaded up and headed for Robinson Flat, Kate was amazed to see the clock on the dash read 1:15. Even though the road was paved, it was slow going with the switchbacks and steep grades.

"Hey," Kate sat up and shouted, "what's going to happen to all that stuff when Rachel's done with it?"

Mollie nodded, liking it that she asked. "On Tuesday I'm packing in a group studying the kit fox. I'll pick it up when we come through."

The lights at Robinson Flat Ranger Station could be spotted now and again as they came down Sunflower Hill in low gear. The official set-up crew was there, busily crossing in front of the lights, doing last-minute preparations. Mollie drove through the main part of the grounds, edging around casually parked trucks and four-by-fours. They drew some mighty curious stares. "Hard to sneak around dragging this thing," Mollie allowed.

At the far side of the vetting area, well away from where the action would be, she parked under a tall ponderosa pine. It didn't take long to set up the one-hour hold for the day's lunch, and they were on their way to the Cedar Springs airport. June would rendezvous with them there sometime after dawn. Then they would go cross-country to intersect the trail at Devil's Thumb.

"Seems we might actually get a couple of hours shut-eye," Mollie yelled.

"Great."

Fifteen

June left her rented car at the Truckee airport, then flew to Foresthill. She would have a couple of hours to catch some zzz's while she waited for Margaret.

At 10:30 June felt a gentle rocking of the plane as Margaret climbed up to the door. "Get your beauty sleep?" she heard as the door opened.

"Raoughaa. I feel like I've been wading face down in a mud hole."

Margaret smiled. She was keyed up and wide awake. "I thought some coffee might be a good idea so I filled up a thermos in town."

"Great." June hauled herself into the truck, managing to get most of the hot brew down before they hit the rough winding roads to Michigan Bluff.

In the light of the Rider's full moon they found a place to set up. Endless gear flowed out of the horse trailer: half a bale of alfalfa hay, lounge chairs, brightly colored buckets, small trunk, cooling sheet for the horse, leg wraps, sponges, and an ice chest with ice for Kestrel's legs and a lunch for the humans.

June stood next to the huge pile of gear ticking off the list as Margaret sorted and organized. "This everything?" she asked.

"No kitchen sink," Margaret said.

While June lashed a tarp over the works Margaret walked around to get a sense of the place—where the horses would be coming in, water location, etc. She found that all the hills resembled an eerie pockmarked moonscape. In the gold rush fever days they had been water cannoned to wash the earth into sluiceways, then their gold was carried away in little leather bags. She could imagine the miners walking off without a look over their shoulders.

Into the blue shadows with bright fluorescent highlights Margaret called out, "Epona, you must be out doing caprioles in the moonlight tonight. Watch over your sisters." Out of the hills a horse neighed. Margaret felt the hair all over her body stand on end.

The crunch of gravelly sand warned her of June's approach. "You moonstruck, girl?"

"A goddess spoke to me."

"Heh heh. Well, I hope she told you to shake a leg."

Margaret related what had happened. "Isn't that strange?" she asked.

A grunted Yeah was all she heard in return.

June was uncomfortable with all the forms of religion she had come across—too much rigidity and ritual. So this talk of goddesses was clear out of her field of experience and she wanted to keep it that way. The tinny slam of the truck door closed the conversation.

Hours of frenetic action later, Margaret slouched in the cramped, hard passenger seat of the plane, the soft drone easing the tension, slipping in and out of an exhausted sleep. As her head would start to sag she would jerk awake, look around with a dazed expression, and say, "You all right, June?" Then the fog would close in again. Great, she thought, I'm going to be a lot of use tomorrow. . .oh, today. She groaned.

"You airsick?"

If only it were that simple, just throw up and be done with it. She rubbed her eyes, then her whole face. "I was just remembering that tomorrow is today and it's going to be a long one."

"Maybe breakfast would help? There's a diner near the airport, open twenty-four hours."

"That's a good idea. I'll probably be hungry once it's put before me."

Margaret looked out of the window, her forehead pressed against the cool glass, and imagined she saw the pine needle-cloaked motel that sheltered Rachel. What was there instead was the little Christmas light decoration that was Truckee, with a garish competitor defining the horizon off to the left. Must be Reno, she thought.

She woke all the way up as the ground rushed toward her, so near in a small plane.

Breakfast did go down mighty easy. Nursing a white plastic cup holding close to a quart of coffee—"large, to go"—Margaret felt her brain gearing up again. When the Piney Peak Motel sign flashed green and orange out of the dark, she called out to June, "Let's see if Kate and Mollie have left a message." June hit the brakes and pulled the Camaro under the arch to park in front of the office sign. Margaret pounded up the stairs and said to the night attendant, in a voice that even to her ears sounded loud and uncontainable by a building, "Any messages for Rachel Duncan?"

The bleary-eyed woman looked at the bank of pigeon holes half-heartedly. After a minute of unfocused attention she said, "What's the number?"

"I don't know. Just give me that piece of paper there." Margaret pointed to the only message in evidence. She reached over the counter and snatched it out of the slot before the night attendant could object. It was brief. *Let 'er rip. Mollie.* Margaret shrieked and threw it in the air. She was out the door, oblivious to the night attendant who was still trying to catch the elusive paper wafting its way toward earth.

"It's on," she crowed, bouncing in her seat.

At the stables Margaret quickly slipped in among the other early morning feeders to find Kestrel curiously watching over the stall door. She welcomed Margaret with a small nicker, not the full rumble from her ribs reserved for Rachel. The grey mare was pleased with the food offering placed before her, grain and a hay net tight with sweet green crackly hay. Margaret hung it high by the open top of the dutch door. A meal with a view.

Nickers came from up and down the shed row as crews arrived to give the early feed.

Margaret slipped back into the Camaro as June tried to tune in a staticky weather report.

In just a few moments they were back at the motel. As they

slowed to drive under the neon arch, Margaret got a glimpse of the tigress manager, her eyes shining through the lit window. Then they were in the soft dark by the tall trees, the resting metallic bodies of the cars guarding each small cottage. An orange light glowed from the last cottage. Margaret started fretting about whether or not Rachel had been able to sleep.

"Always has." June's voice calmed her in its simplicity.

Margaret opened the front door to see Rachel's scrubbed, rested face. "You both look wiped. How did it go? Hear anything from Kate and Mollie?"

An overlapping response of voices followed. "How did you sleep?" "Just got word the mule duo is all set." "Been awake long?" "We're all ready for ya, gal."

Still toweling her hair dry, Rachel poured boiling water from the electric kettle to make coffee. "I was going to try eating some dry cereal and milk but I can't." At Margaret's worried look she said, "Nerves." Rachel poured cream in her coffee, then offered some to June and Margaret. They both made coffeed-out faces.

"You've already fed Kestrel? Yes?" she smiled. "How's my girl?"

"Chomping at the bit about the same as you, I'd say," June replied.

By four o'clock they were getting out of the Camaro in the parking lot at Squaw Valley. Rachel's stomach clutched as she saw the other riders and crews milling in and out of the boundary of stable lights. She quickly became one of them, blending into the watercolors of the scene, a fish in a familiar stream. She wore her electric blue skin-tight riding pants, which definitely added to the piscine look. Her purple-and-blue T-shirt blazed in red letters across her chest, BIG SKY COUNTRY. Her safety helmet cover glowed with the same purple-and-blue stripes accented with a bright red bill. The days of sedate blacks and browns were a thing of the past in horse sport clothing.

June left to verify arrangements with Garcia, while Margaret helped Rachel with Kestrel. To represent Kestrel's ride number, Margaret painted large red zeros on each hip with grease pencil—two startling eyes seen from behind. While Rachel groomed the saddle area in minute detail, Margaret brushed out her silky mane and tail. Rachel could feel the mare's skin quiver over the hard muscles in anticipation. Her ears flicked like butterflies in all directions at once.

Rachel carefully placed the saddle and lightly girthed it up. As she held the bridle up, sorting out all the confusion bridles like to twist themselves into, Kestrel grabbed for the bit before Rachel was ready with it. With a gentle laugh she pushed the mare's head away. "Patience," she advised. Kestrel butted her grey head against Rachel's arm, not about to take the advice. Margaret opened the stall door to let them out. "We still have our warm-ups to do," Rachel said.

"Oh?" Margaret leaned against the stall door. She watched as Rachel took each leg, holding the hoof with one hand, the knee or hock with the other, then drew each leg to its full range of movement.

Between movements and slow breaths Rachel said, "Long-distance runners need to warm up with as little waste of energy as possible. The energy a horse needs to travel a hundred miles could be thought of as a reservoir. You don't just waste it trotting around before the start of a race, but you also don't make the mistake of starting cold. A real set-up for injuries. . . you know all this?" She looked up at Margaret as she set the foot down.

Margaret nodded.

"Have I just been boring? Explaining in great detail something you already know about?"

"Darling, I think you're very sweet. So knowledgeable, capable. Her voice trailed off as their bodies came together flushed with warmth. Rachel pushed away, the glowing nest of hips first, hands from Margaret's waist last.

"These aren't the kind of warm-ups I had in mind for myself."

She glanced at the face of her digital watch. "It's fifteen minutes until the first riders go out. I'd better get going to meet Garcia."

Rachel was back into her business mode, focused entirely on the race. After her stretches she mounted her mare, leaned over to briefly kiss her sweet woman, then was instantly lost in the crowd.

Sixteen

Rachel guided Kestrel into the seething pallet of colors. Even in the half-light they were rich, unadorned horse coats mixed with the adornment of the riders. On a canvas of predawn mist, bright splotches leapt from one part of the painting to another. Appaloosas with thrown spatter spots across their rumps, Pintos daringly hard-edged, Paints gaily three-toned carried their riders' primary colors and blends of turquoise, chrome yellow, and crimson. Soon they would flow westward between the yellow starting flags to pathfind for the sun.

It was time for Rachel to head for the rendezvous place. Kestrel was ready for some starting signal. She barked her snorts in little blasts of air. Totally out of character, she even grabbed the bit and ripped the reins out of Rachel's hands in one long sweep of exuberance. When Rachel indicated a direction and touched her with her calves, the mare responded with a series of stiff-legged crow hops—closer to bucking than she had ever come in her whole life. Rachel grinned and rode her through this show of high spirits.

Bypassing the starting flags to circle around on a ski slope, she and Kestrel were a small escaping blob of flake white leaving the canvas.

It wasn't long before Rachel could hear the first wave of riders. They were being let off in groups of ten, every two minutes. Six pounded by, with one rider desperately trying to use the other horses to block her overeager mount, a horse who hadn't yet learned that the proverbial mountain was still ahead. Soon it would have an education it would never forget.

The labored breathing of a horse being pushed too hard came to her ears. Someone with a race mentality. Top Ten Fever, they called it, the ones who had suffered and recovered, knowing intimately how it distorted your thinking. The heavy breather, a very pretty Appaloosa with white rump spots, flashed by. Rachel was sure that this horse would be waiting at Robinson Flat for a horse trailer to finish the trip to Auburn.

Another horse appeared, this one a too-thin Arabian, its ribs shadowed by the moon, its white-coated body looking like the grim reaper's steed. A bunch of horses was next, the riders chatting amiably; they knew and respected the three-thousand-foot climb in the next four and a half miles.

Then the song of "Buenos dias, Rachel" reached her ears. Kestrel gave a rumbling nicker, liking the sound of Garcia's voice.

"Morning," Rachel said.

"I'll ride with you up to see the sun rise," he said.

They rode companionably side by side, in no apparent hurry. It could have been a day to go check the steers in the high pasture, or ride the line fence in the spring, except for the constant flow of goal-driven riders.

While Rachel knew it was not a section of the trail to make time on, she was curiously observant about her casualness. This was a pass/fail test, and she must pass to win. She thought, I wonder why I want proof? I know I can do it.

Rachel's windbreaker, pulled on at the barn over a light lambswool sweater, was barely enough to cut the rough cold wind. She was glad she had worn the crocheted cotton-and-leather riding gloves Kate had given her for Christmas. They were just warm enough. Must be close to forty degrees, she thought. "Seems to get colder just before dawn, doesn't it?" she said to Garcia.

The trees rapidly thinned out as they reached the tree line. The ones that somehow survived the altitude, winds, and cold appeared to be hanging on by a thread. They looked feeble, stunted, with two or three limbs on the downwind side only. But you knew that they were very persistent Atlas trees, holding up the sky.

The sun came up at their backs, then moved to the left and danced to their right as they made the switchbacks of the rugged trail. The startling blue of Lake Tahoe was like a wedding gift of a blue china bowl with a silver rim. As the morning light softened the lake's edges, the greyish mist changed to pink.

The wind tugged at, then flattened, the windbreaker against Rachel's chest. The wind had a soaring sound this high, as if it weren't too far from its source. The barrenness, made more cold and lonely by the patches of snow still in the hollows, gave the wind a life here.

"Aren't you worried about all those riders ahead of you?" Garcia asked.

"They'll be behind me later on," she said softly.

The horses held a trot over the top of Emigrant's Pass, a wide bare dish with a monument in the middle of it. Kestrel kept one eye and ear on the snapping flag on top of Watson's monument.

"Who the hell was Watson, anyway?" Garcia laughed as they rode by. "Do people stop and read?"

Rachel reined in, the horses halting side by side. "I doubt it with this view as competition."

Off to the west the land was a massive violet and green accordion accented by deep blue canyons and rugged folds of ridges. The sun hadn't reached high enough yet over the Sierra Nevada front to directly light even the tops of the ridges. The half-light gave the ninety-five miles ahead an ominous feel, an eerie beauty.

"Looking at that," Garcia said with a shake of his head to the west, "I don't know whether to be jealous or relieved. Either way, good luck to you."

Rachel bridged the horses with her hand, the shake was firm, both hands rough and friendly. "Thanks," she said. "It does look like we have some traveling to do." She patted her mare, then pulled her glove back on.

"I'll be waiting at the finish line."

"Hope you don't have long to wait," she smiled.

"Si, amiga."

"Adios." She asked Kestrel to move on down the trail. They rapidly dropped out of the thin air, Kestrel eagerly taking the turns at the switchbacks in her best working-the-cows manner.

Rounding a turn Rachel came upon a couple of horses with

their riders dismounted, blocking the trail. One rider was retching dry heaves beside her horse. Rachel called for room to pass.

"Can't you see she's sick?" was the only response.

"Must have eaten something bad last night," the rider added somewhat dreamily.

"Sick or well, you've got to clear the trail," Rachel said. "Get her on her horse and get down to a lower altitude. More than likely it's altitude sickness." The woman she was talking to had a slightly dazed stare. Rachel wasn't certain she understood. "She won't feel better until you get her lower," she said, edging Kestrel by.

"I have a terrible headache," the woman responded, her eyes suddenly turning angry. "Why won't you help us?"

Rachel knew that irrationality was part of the package of altitude sickness. "I have. I've given you good advice. Now you need to follow it. Get on your horses and ride."

She felt some compassion for them and their misery as she rode on down the trail, but not a whole lot. Preparation was crucial, even if it meant arriving a week early to acclimatize. It was the reverse problem for her when she rode in the low lands. Instead of air too thin, it was too thick. She felt strangled by the humidity.

Soon all the altitude gained with so much effort was behind them. Hodgson's cabin lay in a wide valley, but the trail out was steep, rocky, and dangerous. She got off to lead Kestrel and thought, Now we are not talking about a few pebbles in the trail here. These are rocks that take themselves seriously.

Rachel felt playful, her spirit and body strong and eager. Once again in the saddle, she flicked out the reins to give Kestrel her head. The trail snaked out along the sharp edge of a ridge. She was making time now. Other than some low brushy ground cover growing near the ridge crest, the ground was bare, except for the rocks.

Kestrel's ears got sharp and tight, the tips almost touching. Rattlesnake, was Rachel's first fearful thought before she could find the same foreign sound with her ears. With a relief-filled sigh, which she could feel the mare respond to even before she used her voice, she said, "The cameras." So it was with a relaxed and happy smile on her face that she crested Cougar Rock to be immortalized by Janet Reardon of the *Los Angeles Times*. Their eyes met and held as Janet took the camera from her face. "Have'n fun?" Then she spotted the big red zeros on the mare's rump and yelled out, "Hey!"

Janet knew she had found her day's story angle. She ran for her jeep—cameras, light meter, film bag flailing around her neck like some bizarre totem necklace. Planning her route even before she hit the seat of her little dispatcher, she thought, I have to get the story on this chick. Find her crew. Stay ahead of her. This could be the human interest story of the month. She grabbed the map off the seat and read, "Deadman's Flats to. . .ye gods, checkpoint here at. . . ." Her finger rested on the map. "It'll take me as long as it will her." She groaned and tossed the map into the back, retied her bandana over her flame-red hair, and roared off, a rain of gravel spraying up behind her wheels.

Glancing at her wristwatch, Rachel saw it was nearing 7:00. Good time, she thought. We are right on schedule. At the next stretch of rough trail Rachel jumped off and ran beside the mare. It was warming up enough to shed the windbreaker and sweater. She stuffed them in her fanny pack as she ran. She almost missed the first lavender ribbon. Far down the trail she could see the two ribbons warning her that the pit stop was coming up in a few hundred feet. They walked the rest of the way. She heartily approved of Mollie's choice of rest stop location. It was near the end of a section of trail that was dangerous—steep and narrow—and just before it opened up to run along the top of Red Star Ridge. Once she hit that section she could put some speed on all the way to the one-hour hold at Robinson Flat ranger station. The mare would be warmed up but not yet hot and sweaty.

Now was a valuable break she would keep to under ten minutes. Rachel unbuckled and dropped the bit. As Kestrel drank Rachel sponged each leg, carefully checking for bruising, swelling, or cuts. "Great," she crooned to the mare. "Clean, cold, tight." She squirted electrolyte solution, the body's vital salts, into the mare's mouth with the turkey baster, then zipped open the plastic bag and dumped the grain in a bucket. Rachel sponged cold water along neck, chest, inside of the back legs, wherever the big arteries were close to the surface. The more water on the outside, the less Kestrel needed to pull from her system in the form of sweat to keep herself cool. She did a skin pinch on the shoulder, the skin snapping back too fast to count.

By this time the pint of grain was gone, down to the last oat, and Kestrel was making rapid inroads on the hay. Rachel drank as much water as she could, and peed in the bushes. Still geared up, with butterflies in her gut, she stashed the granola bar. Munching the apple, she stood back to look at the whole horse. "You hav'n fun yet?" she asked with a broad grin. She gave the core to the inquiring lips, stowed the full water bottles, and was ready to go. She glanced at her watch. A nine-minute stop, she thought. Just perfect.

She mounted up and they hit the trail. Rachel could feel the mare's eagerness beneath her. Lightly closing her legs, Rachel asked for a canter. Kestrel soared like her namesake.

Suddenly, the road crossing at French Meadows was ahead. This was the first of the "eye-ball" checks, a method of spotting horses in trouble and keeping track of the riders to make sure none got lost. Volunteers, holding clipboards with lists of the numbered riders, waited to check them off. One of them said, "Call your name and number as you go by."

"I'm not an entry," Rachel called out.

"Name," was the terse reply.

"Rachel Duncan, zero," she said, noticing a vaguely familiar woman in a safari jacket, sunglasses perched on her dusty red hair, scribbling in a notebook.

She swept out of the checkpoint in the vanguard of a large group of riders who had finally managed to get their names and numbers straight. She wanted to stay ahead of them, some clear space behind her.

It's started, she thought. *I'll bet that red-haired woman is a reporter, not a commercial photographer.* She worried this bone around in her mind as the mare trotted on.

Rounding a turn, she was suddenly staring at the white tops of four bicycle helmets. Kestrel jumped sideways, narrowly missing the pack, but Rachel's left stirrup caught the outside rider with enough counterforce to flip the mountain bike.

Only a stripped-down moment passed, during which she saw the bike rider was unhurt and simultaneously registered the sound of the nine horses thundering down the trail.

"Clear the trail!" she screamed, with enough urgency to practically lift the bikers up and throw them off the trail. The nine horseback riders sailed past, gaily waving, unaware of the near disaster.

Rachel rode on, wary of blind areas, thinking, I have to remember this area is heavily used. I tend to think of wilderness as meaning no people.

Anger came hot on the heels of relief as she kept finding people on the path: day-hikers, backpackers, and the dreaded mountain bikers. "What do they get out of their wilderness experience, anyway?" she stormed out loud. "Always looking down at the ground! Give me the back of a horse to see the country from."

The deep cool of Duncan Canyon wafted up to them as the trail angled down sharply from the ridge. Kestrel stood in the stream to drink when they reached the bottom, as Rachel threw water on her from a plastic scoop. She figured it was pushing eighty degrees already.

An avalanche of horses coming down the trail made Rachel leap into the saddle to stay ahead of them going up the narrow path out of the canyon. It was getting harder to remain clear of the 249 competitors for the often-narrow trail. Riding along in a friendly chatting group was just not her style. She needed to go at her own pace, to ride her own race.

Seventeen

When they had climbed out of Duncan Canyon Rachel could see the two mountains framing the trail west out of her one-hour hold at Robinson Flat. She put Kestrel into her slow "cooling out" trot, which flushed the system faster than a walk. By the time they reached the ranger station the mare was ready for a slow restful walk, her pulse already dropping.

Cruising over the yellow chalk line that marked the riders in, Rachel set the elapse phase on her watch. The volunteers gave her some very curious looks. One of them asked the head timer in a high nasal voice, "Are we supposed to time her or what?"

The official said, "No," and in a softer voice, "but I am."

Rachel felt a moment of confusion, then spied Margaret as pretty as you please in a large group of ride officials and volunteers, stethoscope around her neck, clipboard in hand.

Rachel slid off the mare, then waited for Margaret to come up to them. "Tired, darling?" Margaret asked, her stethoscope searching behind the mare's elbow for the pulse.

"Me or Kestrel?" Rachel inquired, one eyebrow arched.

"Pulse, sixty. Of course I was asking the horse." She made notes on her clipboard. Stepping back at an angle she counted the respirations at forty. "Very nice. Follow me, Miss."

On the way to their lounging area a breathless woman barged up to them with her notebook out, flipping the pages to find a blank one.

"Excuse me. Excuse me, are you Ms. Duncan?" She turned back a page. "Rachel Duncan?" she finished with satisfaction.

Without waiting for confirmation she asked for an interview with exclusive rights to her story.

"I need to take care of my horse now. Why don't you look me up in about twenty or thirty minutes?"

Janet Reardon was disappointed. "O.K. But you won't talk with anyone first, will you?"

"I'll be talking with my friend here," Rachel said, indicating Margaret with a little sideways nod of her head. The very mild joke was lost on Ms. Reardon.

"Oh, all right." She looked worried, but Rachel thought maybe she always looked that way.

"Who is that?" Margaret asked, as they continued walking.

"Some newshound." Rachel patted her mare on the neck.

"Kestrel looks like she's been for a stroll in the park," Margaret said admiringly. "How's the trail?"

"It's very beautiful, Margaret. You would love it. I wish I could take it slower and explore some of these old mining roads with you."

"Maybe we'll come back some day. Get Mollie to pack us in."

"Yes. This sure isn't the time to do pleasure riding. The trails are thick with people, not just the horses, but bikers." She related the near-miss with the mountain bikes. The story came out with much more flippancy and less fear than she had felt at the time.

"Well," Margaret hesitated, "I guess you wouldn't be here if you weren't challenged." This was a new wrinkle on a known face. "Maybe you like the danger. It's a test for you."

"Oh, sure," Rachel said offhandedly. She heard a shouted greeting and turned to wave at a friend. "Hi, Connie. How's it going?" Margaret moved away, disturbed by her lover's need to be so tough.

The carefully arranged rest area was under a tall ponderosa pine. Waiting for Rachel on either side of a lounge chair were a cooler with a thermos, snack on the lid, and a bucket of water with a towel. An equally inviting place was set up for the mare. A rope had been strung between two trees eight feet apart, a halter dangling from it by a four-foot length of rope. The ground underneath was bedded with straw; water and hay were close at muzzle.

"Mighty fine." Rachel nodded with approval as she replaced Kestrel's bridle with the halter.

There was an extra chair draped with all the needed odds and ends. Rachel picked up a fishnet cooler and threw it over Kestrel's rump and saddle while they both sponged her cool. She left the saddle girthed up tight for ten minutes to give the blood a chance to return slowly.

Rachel kept finding things to do. Margaret suggested a few times that Rachel take it easy. "You can supervise from the chair."

"I'm fine," was the repeated response.

Rachel pulled the saddle, then flooded Kestrel's back with cold water. She moved the fishnet cooler up along the mare's neck, then took the lead rope, intending to walk her around for the final cooling.

"Here, I can do that," Margaret said, reaching for the lead. "You go rest."

"No. I don't need to. I'm feeling just fine. Why don't you take a break? You must be tired." She strolled off with her mare in tow.

Margaret marched over to the lounge chair, letting herself down into it with almost enough force to bend the aluminum frame. She muttered as she glowered in the direction Rachel had taken, "Who does she think she is? Wonder Woman? And the rest of us are her supporting cast. . .wimpy bit players? Why won't she let me do the work I'm here for? No. She has to do it all herself. Damn! Have I made a mistake? Gotten involved too soon?" Sighing, she felt sad, silly, and useless sitting there in the chair intended for Rachel. *Perhaps I'm just cranky from being so tired. I wonder if my period is due.* Her brow furrowed as she tried computing her cycle, coming up with nothing definite enough to hang her cranks on.

Everything was made suddenly more complex by the sight of Rachel returning side by side with Janet Reardon.

Any remnants of cool Margaret might have had left her then. She rose and headed for the outhouse, her usual time-gaining ploy suggested in a workshop led by a reknowned lesbian therapist.

She probably likes that simpering idiot, Margaret thought. *Well, let her show off how capable she is, how she can do it all herself.*

Margaret abruptly came to a full stop. "Whoa," she told herself, laughing, "you're jealous." Once that became clear she knew she could go back. She could deal with that one.

Margaret understood herself well, her good qualities, her flaws. It gave her a strength that wasn't often shaken. In this instance, though, it still left her with the problem, one she could do nothing about: Rachel's need to be what she defined as self-sufficient and tough, the if-you-want-it-done-right-do-it-yourself sort of person.

Margaret could see that Rachel and Janet were quite involved in conversation as she returned to their pit stop. Rachel sat in her lounge chair, Janet in the extra chair, sparking—pencil-chewing, necklace-fiddling energy that matched her flaming hair.

This was an interview Margaret was glad she had missed. She pulled her stethoscope out of her suddenly dumpy-feeling overalls. It was easy to absorb herself in Kestrel's vital signs. In her notebook she wrote, pulse thirty-eight, respirations sixteen. She shook down the thermometer and gently slid it, lubricated with a little spit, into Kestrel's anus. She whiled away the time with her back to the newshound and the star, waiting for the mercury to register in the fine glass tube. Finally she brought it out, wiped the traces of manure off on her coverall leg with a swift thought about elegance, then wrote down 102.2 degrees and the time in her notebook. Time to get rid of this woman, she thought with a deep touch of pleasure.

In her best New England upper-class snob voice she turned to them to say, "Rachel has twenty minutes before she needs to leave so it's time to close this interview."

Reardon studied this interloper, flicked off her lens cap, and clicked the shutter as she said, "Mind if I get a few shots of the crew?"

"Not at all."

She stood back to include Kestrel.

"Bye now," Margaret added pointedly.

Recognizing a superior force, Janet Reardon of the *Los Angeles Times* retreated.

Margaret stomped over to the cooler to fish out some lemonade for herself. "Don't you want anything?" she asked Rachel crossly.

"No, darling. Sit here beside me." She patted the chair, still warm from Ms. Reardon's rear.

Margaret thought briefly of rejecting it, then sat like her Victorian-influenced New England aunts sat, carefully arranging her coveralls.

"What's wrong?" asked Rachel.

After a brief winnowing of her feelings, Margaret responded. "I get the feeling that it makes no difference to you whether I'm here or not."

Rachel tried to interrupt, a hurt look on her face. "Of course I want you here—"

Margaret's raised hand stopped her. "I am not talking about company. I'm talking about your not being able to give over control, your lack of trust that I can adequately care for Kestrel, your need to do it all yourself to prove how strong you are." Margaret was surprised at her frankness. She tried to clarify how Rachel's actions affected her. "You see, I end up feeling kind of helpless and femmy, so that you can maintain your idea of yourself. That way we both lose."

Rachel's eyes got a distant veiled look. "I'll think about this. I can't take it in right now." She dunked the towel in the bucket, wiped it over her face and arms, then turned to Margaret. "I thought you might be jealous of Janet."

"I was, briefly. Did you want me to be?" At Rachel's flushed face, Margaret laughed. "Darling, I won't experience the poison of jealousy in my relationship anymore. I will just leave."

"I don't want you to leave," Rachel said sadly.

They sat quietly looking at each other.

At this point in the tense conversation Kestrel lay down on the straw with a soft groan. Margaret put her hands on the arms of the chair to stand. Rachel, reading Margaret's anxiety, quickly said, "It's all right. She's not having colic. That's why I wanted the straw. She usually takes a nap at the one-hour holds." She went on conversationally, glad of something else to talk about. "I think that is part of why she does so well on these rides, that she can rest so deeply." Glancing at her watch she added, "I'll get her up in about ten minutes. Have they pulled any horses yet?"

"Yes," Margaret answered, relieved, too, at the change of subject. "Somebody on a very skinny grey Arabian got into an argument with the judge when he was not allowed to go on. Anybody could see there was nothing left in the horse." Rachel flashed on the memory of the horse in the moonlight. "I saw a couple of riders withdraw right before you got here. Wouldn't you like a sandwich or something?" Margaret said, rummaging in the cooler. "There's tunafish and let's see. . . peanut butter and peach jam."

"No thanks, Margaret. I'll probably want something by the time we hit Michigan Bluff. The thought of food still turns my stomach."

Kestrel stretched all four legs out straight, then neatly folding her front legs under herself, rolled over on her chest. Taking in her surroundings, she seemed to remember what she was here for. She rose to her feet in that impressive way horses have of suddenly becoming very large. After shaking herself like a dog she looked over at Rachel. If she had had eyebrows, they would have been raised, questioning her person why she was lounging in that plastic chair when she could be on her own mare's back.

The two women smiled at each other, the sense of connection returning, then stood to gear up for the next stage of the ride. While Rachel stashed water bottles in her fanny pack and started her slow stretches, Margaret got out a fresh, clean saddle pad and worked on getting Kestrel ready.

Rachel kept wanting to check on everything Margaret did, or do it herself, but she had been hit pretty hard by the seriousness of Margaret's statement. Did she really believe that she was the only one who could do it right? Feeling somewhat sober and subdued, she took the reins of the prepared steed from Margaret.

As Rachel put on her helmet, Margaret briefed her about the location of the crew stop that had been prepared by the rest of the gang. She read off the weather forecast from her notebook and some warnings about trail conditions on the far side of El Dorado Canyon.

Mounting up, Rachel reached her fingers out to touch Margaret lightly on the top of her head. Gathering the reins, she said, "Thank you for doing this for me. I'll think about what you said."

She set her digital watch as she headed for the yellow chalk line.

Eighteen

The reassuring presence of Kestrel beneath her gave Rachel a sense of power. She could feel the surge of energy, the light connection of that living force to herself, through subtle shifts in weight, the slightest closing of a leg, a touch on the neck or a soft word. Right at that moment, it seemed all she wanted from living.

Together they rode up over a steep grade out of Robinson Flat, then along the hog back of Cavanaugh Ridge. Now they were traveling through the heart of the California gold fields. She remembered the map covered with little crossed picks and shovels as thick as ants around here. Dirt roads, barely more than trails, led off in all directions to the old digs.

Cavanaugh Ridge was like a freeway after the narrow ups and downs of the first part of the trail. Kestrel stayed to a steady trot with occasional breaks into a canter. The miles slipped by. Soon she was swinging by the "eyeball" check at Dusty Corners. The mare was full of energy. After a short stop wading and drinking in Bear Trap Creek, the blast of heat back up on top of the ridge was daunting. It took Rachel back briefly to a memory of fighting a forest fire in the Little Belts. The fire had been more than heat alone—a palpable animal, huge, hungry, the breath rank.

She took a bottle out of her red fanny pack, squirted water into her mouth and under her helmet, then emptied it over Kestrel's already dry neck and mane. She put the empty back, then looked at her watch. Soon she would be resupplied.

The checkpoint at Last Chance swept by in a heat wave blur.

She got a glimpse of Janet Reardon's red hair arching out in a halo from behind her camera. Kestrel's trot was strong. She waved in the direction of Janet's camera, a self-confident, even cocky, gesture.

The trail led down a long hill to the foot bridge over the American River. This was a long suspension bridge with spidery cables weaving down to support it. It was very narrow, only wide enough for one horse. If Rachel had not crossed this bridge two years ago on a training clinic she knew she would have been freaked. All fears to the contrary, it was steady and, if one could only keep one's cool, the horse would take it in stride.

Reaching it, Rachel found a rider trying to lead her horse across. The horse, smart enough to believe his rider's body language, refused. When Rachel dismounted next to them the horse instantly relaxed from the comfort of company. Herd instinct is very strong, and although horses are willing to accept their human as sufficient herd for short periods of time, they always heave a sigh of relief to have another equine around. Understanding this and working with it was one of the elements that made Rachel a very good trainer.

"How long have you been here?" she asked.

The frazzled woman said, "It feels like days." She glanced at her watch, "But it's only been twenty minutes. I thought he would cross behind another horse, but he still refuses. My friends rode on five minutes ago and he has been a maniac since then."

"That's a long time." Rachel agreed. "Why don't you blindfold him with your T-shirt, walk him in a circle, then follow us across? I don't think he'll realize when he's on the bridge. It's steady, you know."

The young woman's face flooded with relief. She pulled her T-shirt over her head shyly, trying to keep her arms crossed over her white cotton bra. Rachel felt sad to realize the embarrassment she seemed to feel, here in the wilderness with another woman.

It worked. Rachel walked in a circle leading Kestrel, then straight onto the bridge, the little chestnut gelding following closely.

Looking down was like being in an airplane, seeing the tops

of clouds out of the window with an occasional glimpse through cracks of the dark earth sickeningly far below. Only these weren't clouds, they were the tops of trees underfoot, and way down below rushed the Middle Fork of the American River, so far below it was silent.

Rachel thought about the notorious No Hands Bridge near the end of the ride and wondered how this team would cope with it. Hundreds of feet high, it crossed a river-filled rock-walled canyon in a series of bare concrete arches. Built originally for trains, it was narrow, had no guard railing of any kind, and though it was wide enough for two horses, most rode right down the middle, eyes front.

Once across the suspension bridge Rachel mounted up and rode on, leaving the woman to rearrange her attire in private. Coming to a fork she took the left uphill one: Devil's Thumb was at the top of a steep canyon. She gave a swift double-checking glance to the right fork bearing north, noticing that there were no yellow trail markers in this section. They should have marked this part more carefully, she thought. More tracks appeared to be leading off to the left.

A growl rumbled up out of her gut, and the thought of the granola bar in her pack brought a flood of saliva to her mouth. Margaret had told her the crew stop would be set up at the small spring just past the suspension bridge. There would be something invitingly cool, offered to her from an ice chest. Worth waiting for. Hawklike, her eyes scanned ahead for lavender ribbons.

A couple of riders swept past her. The trail kept going up. She dismounted to ease the mare, hungrily searching the trees for the markers. She knew it was possible to miss one, but all three? This must not be Devil's Thumb, she thought, about to turn around.

Up ahead she saw some backpackers. She would ask them— they were usually into maps. Scrambling up the trail she called out to them, "Wait!" Just beyond the hikers she could see another rider leading his horse down toward them. "I'll be damned. Dwight Newton," she muttered under her breath.

As she caught up with the backpackers she froze at the sight of a neatly bundled shock of yellow ribbons festooning one of their packs.

"Oh," she groaned, "you've been taking down all the trail markers."

"Trail markers?" said the tall man with a beard, wet bandanna tied around his sweaty neck, knobby knees peeking out from below khaki shorts. "Aren't these Desert Storm ribbons?" His confusion was only momentary, quickly replaced by righteousness. "They are plastic," as if that explained everything.

Rachel was on the verge of explosion. Hunger had caught up with her, increasing her irritability and impatience. "Who do you think you are? God's gift to the environment? There is a horse race going on. I've gone out of my way and a lot of others, too, I expect." She felt herself shaking, close to rage.

At this tense moment Dwight joined them, leading his big bay gelding. He had a map in his hand and a puzzled look on his face. "Hi, Rachel. Look, do you know where we are?" He pulled a big white handkerchief out of his hip pocket to wipe his sweaty brow.

His horse rolled his eyes and reacted as though he were about to be struck. Grunting in fear, he ran back, breaking away from Dwight. He ran up the trail, his flight aggravated by Dwight's bellowed demand to "Come back here."

The backpackers stared with curiosity at Dwight roaring at his now-absent horse. The tall man turned to Rachel to say, "Well, aren't you going to do anything about catching your friend's horse?"

"I didn't get him into this mess," she said to the backpacker. "And Dwight, if you wouldn't yell at and rough up your horses, they wouldn't run away from you."

Dwight's only response was a blank, cold stare.

Two riders came into view. "We saw a horse go by but couldn't catch it. Anybody hurt?" A woman and her teenage daughter stopped beside them. "We just figured out we are lost. Oh, shit—" she said, catching sight of the collected yellow ribbons gracing the top of the pack. The hiker cringed, expecting another onslaught, but was saved by Dwight's demand that someone get his horse. All were silent as his audacious arrogance echoed into the air.

Much as Rachel despised him she could not refuse to catch his horse. This, an old western unwritten law, was akin to throwing out a life preserver to a drowning sailor. It would be a challenge to make up this wasted time, but she figured she could get this job done and be back on the trail fast.

The teenage girl said, "Want some help? Hey, Mom, she needs some help catching her friend's horse."

Hearing Dwight referred to as her friend twice in a mere five minutes was the last straw. "I don't need any help," Rachel snapped. She knew she had squelched the kid in her irritation but was certain she could catch the horse faster alone. She mounted and rode on up the trail, leaving them all behind.

This was clearly not Devil's Thumb. The trail leveled, then veered sharply south. Kestrel's ears focused on a clump of junipers. It took a few minutes of studying them before she could make out the shape of the bay horse hiding there. He warily watched them. The moment she moved Kestrel forward he burst from cover to tear off in a plunging downhill scramble.

Damn. This is going to take all day. Rachel indicated to Kestrel that the bay was their quarry and the mare responded with her best herding action. She worked the bay toward an eroded bank that became increasingly steep as they went downhill.

Up ahead a couple of giant ponderosa pines had come loose, falling down the bank and blocking the narrowing draw. They conveniently formed a makeshift three-sided corral.

"Gotcha now," Rachel said with a small, satisfied smile. She halted Kestrel far enough back not to crowd the frightened gelding. The bay's ears were swiveling in a nervous way, seeking out escape. His body was trembling, sweat sticking to his coat in thick, gummy patches. His eye had a glazed look that wasn't all fear, indicating the horse was seriously dehydrated.

This horse is in trouble, Rachel thought. "Easy, now," she crooned. "It's going to be all right." As she spoke she edged Kestrel nearer, moving her sideways to keep the gelding blocked.

Maneuvering close enough to reach the reins dangling from the bridle, she leaned down, putting all her weight in the right stirrup. Slowly she reached out, grasping one rein. Almost as soon as she had it in her hand she knew she had moved too soon.

The gelding grunted in panic, reared up, then bulldozed his way past Kestrel's head. Rachel let go of the rein, recognizing superior motivation; she was not about to get herself into trouble trying to restrain him.

Moments later, with a shock, she found herself pulled from the saddle and dragged beneath Kestrel's chest.

The next few seconds were a chaotic blend of agony and surprise as she felt her clothes—T-shirt, lycra pants—shredded from her, the skin taking the ripping of rocks, sand, and tree roots. She felt an odd puzzlement about finding herself in this present reality. *How did this happen? It couldn't be.*

Rachel could feel herself dragged by the rein. It seemed to be attached somehow to her fanny pack. She worked desperately to unbuckle it. *Why didn't the damn horse stop?* He was dragging her from the bit in his mouth. He must have a mouth like iron. Before she could unfasten the buckle she felt the crashing connection of hooves laced with iron. Her helmet split like a coconut, and she lost consciousness.

The horse was in a state of terror. As he ran he kicked out at the thing dragging along behind him, desperately trying to free himself. He connected. The thing broke free and now only a small fanny pack chased him over the rocks. A quick snap and he was free even of that. Kestrel ran with him, picking up the fear the bay carried. It never registered on her that Rachel was the thing sliding down the embankment. The horses ran on.

Nineteen

No one had said anything for at least fifteen minutes. June paced out to the trail again. She looked at her watch. *Noon. Rachel should have been through here at least an hour ago.*

Mollie, lying on the ground, back against a tree, one boot resting on the other, eyed her mules from the shade of her hat. Sound asleep. Just like she wanted to be. She wished Rachel would get on through this crew stop so she could truck her mules out and find a nice soft motel room bed. She was too old to cuddle up with tree roots anymore.

Kate caught June's worried look. "Something's wrong," Kate said. "We can't hang around here all afternoon waiting. I've got to do something. Look, why don't I ride up to Last Chance and at least find out when—and if—they passed that checkpoint."

Once it had been admitted that things weren't all right, there was a sense of relief in the action. June firmly supported Kate's suggestion.

Mollie pushed her hat back and nodded her agreement. She rose without a word to get Friar ready, then changed her mind. "Take Chalk, he's faster."

The grey mule caught Kate's sense of urgency. He pawed restlessly, waiting for a few riders to cross the suspension bridge. Climbing up the long, steep trail out of the canyon it seemed to Kate she was riding a Steelhead trout, fighting the current of riders flowing toward her.

On reaching Last Chance, Kate quickly learned that her team had passed through there at 10:09, "going strong." "Rachel must be lost," she said, fighting back her other fears.

One of the officials offered to radio ahead to the Deadwood check to see if she had passed through there. The large heavy man with soft folds in his neck and kindness in his eyes leaned his ear to the receiver on the two-way radio. "Umn-huh, ummmn, yes, over and out." His face had added a somber look. "Her horse is there. A grey with red zeros on the hips?" he asked for confirmation. He got a shocked nod from Kate's paling face, then continued. "Turned up with another horse, a bay gelding, around 11:15. Timers weren't exact. The horses came in with a group of riders who couldn't tell them much. Sorry." He spoke with compassion, aware of the effect this had on her. Two riders lost, more than likely hurt, with a lot of territory to search.

Kate stood frozen while action continued around her, riders arriving, getting checked out. Contained in her still body was a mind that raced, forming a search plan. She touched the radio operator on the arm to get his attention, then asked him to raise Michigan Bluff and page Dr. Margaret Carson. Fleetingly she thought about leaving a message so she could get back to the others and start the search. No, she thought, too easy to get messages garbled over the two-way radio. She would wait to talk with her directly.

Kate remembered reading in the Western States Trail Ride Information Packet that riders were responsible for themselves. Any rider lost would have to wait to be found until after the ride was finished, as far as management was concerned.

It was true, Kate thought. They couldn't drain off ride workers to try to locate imbeciles who strayed off the trail. She paced back and forth. Except for Rachel. It suddenly didn't make as much sense to her as it had when she first read it. The rule seemed pretty heartless. Restless and anxious, she waited for Margaret's call to come through. Every time the radio crackled she tensed to watch for a sign that it was for her.

Hanging out at the open air radio station beside the Michigan Bluff headquarters building, Janet Reardon heard it first. She was there to do just that—get the first word on an interesting story. Feeling torn between locating Margaret or missing something else juicy coming in on the radio, she flagged down a kid.

She knew the kid could get to Margaret faster than the slow grind of officialdom. When she offered him a quarter for the job, he screwed up his face at her and smirked, "Where are you from, lady, the dark ages?"

"Oh," she said as she fished a dollar out of her light tan designer slacks.

Resting in the lounge chair where she could see the timer's yellow line onto the grounds, Margaret was not worried. Rachel had estimated her arrival time between 12:30 and 1:00. It was fifteen minutes to one now. When the boy told her some lady at the radio tent wanted her to come there, she ignored the message once she figured out it came from Janet Reardon. Probably setting up some photo opportunity, she thought.

Fifteen minutes later a jeep drove slowly through the grounds, megaphone blaring out, "Dr. Carson, please come to the office." That brought her out of her chair and heading for the office at a gallop.

Janet waited by the radio tent. When she saw Margaret running toward her she raised the camera. *Click.*

"What's going on?"

First Janet took a picture, then she answered. "Her horse turned up at Deadwood without her." *Click.*

"Stop that!" Margaret demanded. "Tell me what you know. Where is Rachel? Is she hurt? How did you hear this?"

"Over the two-way radio from Deadwood. That's all I know," Janet reluctantly admitted.

Margaret took the four stairs to the office in one stride, but was instead rapidly escorted to the radio tent by a concerned official who explained to her they could not spare anyone for a search at this time. "Tomorrow we could help you out."

She waited, stunned, while the radio operator raised Last Chance. "Putting through a call to Kate Singer. Over." A bird's nest of static filled the air, then a croak. "Over." He handed the headset to Margaret.

"Hello? Kate?"

After a few fits and starts they managed to work out the radio transmitting etiquette essential to its use. Margaret agreed to Kate's plan. Mollie and June could look between Last Chance and the footbridge, while she would meet Margaret at Deadwood to search that section of trail.

"How long do you think it will take you to get to Deadwood?" Kate asked.

"I've got to get a ride." Her eyes locked on Janet. "I'll be there in about an hour."

It was a mere twelve miles by trail, but because El Dorado Canyon lay between, it would be a drive of nearly forty miles. They signed off.

Margaret grabbed Janet's arm. "Get me to Deadwood, fast. You've got a jeep and a press pass." Her eyes searched the depths of the reporter, sniffing under the hard outer shell.

"O.K.," Janet said, feeling compelled by Margaret's urgency.

"Take me to our crew spot first. I've got to get some things. They both jumped into the jeep. Janet knocked down the visor to expose her press pass, their ticket to the "off limits" roads.

While Margaret dashed around gathering together everything she thought they might possibly need, the little jeep dispatcher idled like a semi in a diner parking lot. Janet kept a nervous tapping on the dashboard, her silver wrist bangles an impatient background rhythm. She ended her concert with a rude jab to the horn. Janet put it in gear as Margaret tossed her bundle in the back, her boot hitting the accelerator the same time that Margaret reached the seat next to her. Janet peeled out of the grounds just under the speed of reckless, then floored the accelerator after making, barely, the turn up the Chicken Canyon road. She appeared to have a total disregard for mechanical life expectancy as well as anything that might take it into its head to cross the road.

By the time the small end of the V had been reached at Westville, Margaret could feel her arms trembling from the strain of holding herself in the open-sided jeep. She was sure that if she loosened her grip even for a moment she would be thrown from the vehicle on a curve or a jolting bump. Arriving at Deadwood, the utter relief of Janet's rut-digging stop did little to keep her biceps from dissolving in a screaming pool of jelly.

Workers bustled with clipboards in arms, stethoscopes slung

around necks, all their attention on the riders and horses coming into Deadwood. Kestrel stood, tied under a tree with a bucket of water near her. Margaret had held onto a fragment of hope until then that it would not be Rachel's mare. That somehow it was a mistake, the worst of it being that Rachel would arrive at Michigan Bluff without a crew to assist her.

But it was Kestrel. Margaret walked over to her, checked her all over to make sure she was unhurt, then stood quietly looking at her.

Janet's voice cut sharply into her thoughts. "You think she is going to tell you anything?"

"I wish she could."

Margaret turned to find some worker who might have information. She asked a woman standing nearby about the horse that came in with Kestrel. The woman called out, "Jack, what's the story on that guy's bay horse? You know, the one that came in with the grey?" She motioned over her shoulder. "These folks are trying to find out what happened."

Jack and his P&R partner came over to them. "What was the guy's name," he said, looking questioningly at his co-worker as he screwed up his face. "Oh, yeah, Dwight Somth'n."

Margaret groaned. "You know him?" Jack asked.

"Slightly."

"Well, it seems he ran up about an hour or so ago, grabbed his horse from Sally." He pointed to a short blonde woman. "Didn't even thank her for taking care of his horse. Came in badly dehydrated. He just jumped on and rode off. We got his number, though. Sally asked him what happened to the other rider. He never even looked at her, she said."

"He must still be at Michigan Bluff. I've got to get some information from him before he leaves there."

"Yeah, I can see why. No telling where your friend is in all this country." He looked around, somehow emphasizing the vastness. "I'll bet you're worried about him."

"Her. Yes, I am. Thanks for your help."

Jack pointed out the radio operator set up under some trees, "Talk to Tracy. Hope you find your friend before dark."

Margaret made her way to the radio operator, as Jack had indicated, with fear snapping at her heels. She had to wait for a tall brunette woman wearing a Ham Is Best T-shirt to finish her two-way conversation. "Tracy," Margaret asked forcefully, "could you raise Michigan Bluff and have rider number—" she frantically searched her memory—"number fifty-eight held. He might have information on a lost, possibly injured, rider."

Janet continued to scribble in her notebook as she followed Margaret's attempts to piece events together.

While Tracy worked her dials on the radio, Margaret spotted Kate riding up on a fine grey mule. Kate raised her hand in a silent greeting, then tied the mule up next to Kestrel. After a quick inspection of the mare she came over to stand near Margaret. "Took me forever. It's not far as the crow flies, but that mule there isn't a crow. Find out anything?"

"Remember Dwight Newton? You must have met him on the rides."

"Oh, yeah. Figgy."

"It was his horse Kestrel came in with."

"Oh." Kate went over to the mare like she too expected to get it from the horse's mouth. Kestrel nuzzled Kate, blowing her warm breath against her already sweaty shirtfront.

Kate—cold, angry, thoughtful—strode back to Margaret's side. "So this has something to do with that bastard. Where is he?" Her eyes searched for him.

"He came in over an hour ago, got on his horse, and rode out. The radio operator is trying to locate him at Michigan Bluff."

Tracy's face flushed red after listening to the other end of the radio. She nodded her head. "Yup, yup, uh-huh." Then, after a while, "Out." She turned to the listening women to say, "This guy, Dwight Newton, is claiming your friend Rachel Duncan deliberately spooked his horse, then chased it up the trail. He yelled at her to stop, but she ignored him, leaving him stranded in the wilds. He hiked on to the nearest checkpoint, found his horse, and rode on." She smiled in an embarrassed sort of way, aware that she was in the middle simply by virtue of relaying this outrageous story.

"Poppycock," Margaret said, her eyes round and hard like glass trade beads.

Kate said, "Maybe this happened near here."

"All he would say was that it happened before Devil's Thumb. Oh, another thing that's interesting is that the veterinarian pulled his horse from competition for severe bit injuries. He claims it was your friend's fault. He has had support from two other riders for at least part of his story."

Kate and Margaret stared at each other silently, knowing there was much more to tell.

"There's a woman standing behind you taking notes," Kate stated, close to Margaret's ear.

"A reporter," Margaret said absently.

She thanked Tracy, then went to her pile of stuff. Kate helped her sort out the things they might need into two bundles to tie behind the saddles.

"I'm going to have to ride Kestrel," Margaret said. "There's nothing else. Do you think she's too tired?"

"Hell," Kate answered with a snort, "she's only gone fifty miles."

Ye gods, it occurred to Margaret. Distance, like time, must be relative.

Suddenly, Margaret remembered Janet. "Are you coming?" she asked briskly.

Click, click. "No. I don't do well in the jungle." She pulled a designer hanky out of a pocket to wipe her brow, then put the lens cap on her camera. Clearly, she had to find another story. She slung herself into her jeep and drove away.

Margaret was disgusted. *A powerhouse with no staying power.*

A clicking sound, or was it ticking, came into a back part of Rachel's consciousness. The travel clock. It was so close to her ear. The room was so hot. These motels were so stuffy. She could hardly breathe. She had to wake up enough to turn the electric blanket down. She opened her eyes a tiny slit, then shut them again because the lamp was glaring in her eyes. *Too bright.* Opening her eyes very cautiously again, she could see something blurry on the pillow by her head. Working hard at pulling the images together into a single shimmering one, she saw what it was. Something like a baby porcupine. *No. Impossible.* She tried again and saw that it was her own hand with pine needles bristling out of red-brown places on it. She tried to drag it closer. The burning, gripping pain of this simple request for movement sent the motel far away, leaving her alone on the western slope of some ridge with the sun trying to turn her into jerky.

"Kestrel," she called out. Only the beetles and the grasshoppers answered with their little metallic clicks and ticks. Knowing her tongue had been a failure at speech, she moved everything in her mouth around, checking out its range of movement and her ability to coordinate. Pretty poor, she thought. One of the problems was that she didn't have any spit left. She would drink some water, then things would work better.

She struggled to free the hand that was trapped under her body. The effort took all of her concentration. Once it was lying beside her she rested a bit before she would ask her hand to reach behind her to get the water from her fanny pack.

Oh, where was Kestrel? Somehow, if Kestrel would just show up, she could get back on and they would complete the ride. She was unable to accept that she was really hurt. She would reach back, get the water bottle, have a long cold drink, then get up and find her mare. *Right.*

Reaching back, she was amazed to not find it. The effort and the disappointment sent her back into unconsciousness.

It was a more humble Rachel who awoke later. She was beginning to appreciate that her life was in danger. The sun blazed full on her, radiating up from the western side of the ridge she was on. I can't keep lying here in the sun, she thought feebly. Moving her tongue around in her mouth again to prepare it for shouting, she found she couldn't get it to work. The dried cracked lips were hardened like papier mâché—they came near each other but were not really designed to be functional. In spite of the pain from her body she lifted her head, trying to find some shade she could crawl to. With her good hand she pulled herself downhill to the shelter of a creosote bush. Then she slipped back into her painless dark.

She came screaming up out of her peaceful unconscious minutes later, feeling something gripping her back with a stabbing shock of pain that sent her reeling downhill. She even used her porcupine hand to propel herself. Slewing around, she faced her attacker: a carrion-eating magpie who wanted to make her its supper.

She sang in her mind, trying to make the sounds, trying to appease the bird. *Hush now, baby, don't say a word, Momma's gonna buy you a mockingbird, and if that mockingbird don't sing. . . . No, no, that wasn't it. What was the other song Mother used to sing? All the pretty little horses. . . that one.* Her eyes grew frightened. *What was that about, the part about pecking out the eyes of the lamb?*

She found herself gasping for breath, sobs wracking her body worse than the pain in her torn skin and muscles.

Finally there she was. She knew where she was now. Her mother had kept her home from school because she had a fever. She was sitting beside her, a concerned expression on her face, holding a glass full of lemonade with beads of cool sweat running down its side like tiny snails.

Rachel felt a sweet, deep, nurtured feeling in the base of her gut. Her mother would take care of her until she could get up and run around and get her own lemonade. Suddenly the menacing presence of her father filled the frame of the door. She did not know what she had done to make him so angry. He said in an unpleasant voice, "You're treating her like a baby, spoiling her. You'll turn her into a weakling." He stepped into the room abruptly, grabbed the lemonade out of her mother's hand, then hurled it across the room. The glass smashed against her bookcase, leaving a slightly sticky reminder for years to come. "Get up," he said disdainfully to Rachel, "there is nothing wrong with you."

She tried to. She tried really hard, whimpering, but the most she could manage was a twitchy, crawly motion. The roots under her breasts and the sand abrading her cheek took her out of her bedroom like a time machine.

The magpie sat a few feet away, dressed for dinner in black-and-white tuxedo, waiting, chattering at her. It came to her that this bird was here to tell her that she was very close to becoming meat. Soundless sobs paired with waterless tears were the first outward sign of her lifelong inward mourning. For the first time in her life she was crying for herself, for all she had lost: her parents, Amy, her teenage freedom. Shoved into being a responsible adult before she was done with being a child. None of this was articulated in her brain. Her tears had been shut away over a lifetime to be cried later, the accumulation too great to be done casually, eventually becoming too frightening to be done at all.

She felt helpless for the first time since the overwhelming helplessness of being small. She knew that she had become super rancher so that she would never again need anyone. Besides, she wasn't about to be one of those weak, crying, babylike women. Men never sniveled, never really needed anybody. She knew now they were wrong. A crack had opened up in that belief, letting in feelings like fresh air.

There was a fuzzy edge to everything. Her brain felt like some one-celled amoeba testing out a primitive form of locomotion. It pushed its way through tissue membranes of consciousness, trying to reach the surface of a sea, one that might be in a test tube over a lab burner.

The magpie chattered again. Very close. I'm dying, Rachel thought with shock. Trying to sustain this moment of clarity, she lifted her head to look around. She used the pain this time to stay alert. She knew her chances were running out like the final grains of sand in an hourglass. She was on a slope, she thought. Often there were creeks in the bottoms of draws around here. She must get to water to live. It had to be downhill. Fighting off the sucking pull of the bliss of unconsciousness, she kept her head downhill to make what little fluid there was in her system available to her brain.

The magpie flew a short flight beside her, flashing its carnivorous eye and its long black-and-white tail. Keeping pace with her, it hopped along downed timber, perched on rocks, sat on a bobbing creosote bush branch. A reminder to keep moving. Rachel started to smile at it, thanking the bird for keeping her going. It was doubtful the magpie would recognize her facial expression for a smile.

Her lips had vertical cracks in them and were drawn away woodenly from her teeth. The whites of her eyes were yellowish; the mucous membranes around them, drained of even the tiny amount of fluid sent to these vital organs, were a dark brick red.

During one of her brief moments of lucidity, she pinched the skin of her arm to check it for dehydration. She stared at it, waiting for it to flatten out, but the small sharp ridge of skin stayed in its little pup tent shape.

It was fortunate she could not see her back. It had taken the full force of the horse's powerful strength as it pulled her across sharp rocks. Pieces of her T-shirt were fused by crusts into her shoulder blades. The rest of the shirt had been torn away, made into rags on the mountainside. Her bra's racing straps were still looped over the tops of her arms, now acting more like a necklace than mammary support. As she half crawled, half slid, cracks opened in the red crusts like a newly formed planet's lava beds. Her blood was thick and slow, seeping down her lycra pants, torn back along one leg. A long red racing stripe that hadn't been there in the morning accented one leg.

The earth started moving underneath her, sliding, carrying her along in a cascade over a bank and into shockingly cold water. Even before she could get her head above water to breathe she was sucking in deep hungry gulps, filling her stomach with the frigid shock of it. All of her awareness was focused on the cold column from mouth down, the sensation of the water going down, filling each thirsty cell.

She was brought violently to her knees, rising up out of the creek to retch up the water she had just swallowed. Easing onto her back she let the water wash and numb her as she floated in and out of consciousness.

Twenty

M ollie sat beside the trail, gazing off to the west. Her map tube rested against her right knee, unopened. Her eyes were in narrow slits, focused in an unfocused way on the nearest trail marker. Her hat crowned the top of a nearby stump. A slight breeze in the canyon lifted her hair gently.

June waited with Mollie under some trees while the mules rested. Since one o'clock they had searched the trail between Last Chance and the footbridge over the American River. Nothing. No clue, nor even any ideas about what might have happened.

"When in doubt, give instinct a free rein," was a Mollie-ism. She was doing that now, falling back on a kind of animal sorting of the information in her head.

June snatched up the map tube. "Well, it's almost 5:30. I'm not just going to sit and do nothing. I won't give up on Rachel. Where are we, anyway?" She spread Mollie's Forest Service map out on the ground. "This map is a disgrace. Why don't you get a new one?" she demanded.

To Mollie, at that moment, June was no more irritating than the magpie on a tree limb opposite her. In great detail June explained her plan to do a grid search of the area. Mollie stood, put on her hat, and was in the saddle without a word, Friar trotting down the trail and over the suspension bridge as if it were a Central Park bridle path.

Mounting her mule, Sherpa, June stuffed the maps into the tube as she rode. She called out, cross and irritable, "Why can't we go about this in a sensible fashion? Mollie, will you stop?"

"No," Mollie called back, turning in her saddle. "Can't ya get that ornery, pampered, half-ass daughter of a horse out of first gear?"

Trotting up beside Mollie, June looked her full in the face. "I'm not going to keep pairing up with you if you start cuss'n at me or the mules. I think we should—"

"But don't you see?" Mollie interrupted, "we've been wasting our time. She can't be on that side of the river," gesturing back behind her. "The horses would have gone back to Last Chance. They wouldn't have crossed the suspension bridge on their own. Not even the mules would have. They wouldn't have shown up at Deadwood. She has to be over here somewhere."

June looked back behind her at the high cable-hung bridge with its tiny spider walkway, welcome only to a person or horse with aerialist aspirations. "You're right, Mollie."

Trotting next to Mollie, June pointed ahead and yelled," Look!"

Mollie tried to see what June was pointing at. "What?" she asked impatiently. "There's nothing there."

"That's right." For the first time all afternoon there was a smile on June's face. "The trail markers are gone. Someone has taken them down, and I'll bet you anything Rachel took that trail off to the left. She would have been near the front of the pack at that point and the trail much less marked up by all these tracks."

They brought the mules to a halt at the Y in the trail. Mollie nodded. "That would explain why she never reached our pit stop. It's only about a hundred feet up the trail from here. Well, what are we wait'n for? Let's ride."

"Just hold your horses, dear. It's almost six. We have to leave a note for the others. It will only take a few minutes to ride up there."

"All right," was Mollie's reluctant response. Now that she knew where she was going, she didn't want to be slowed down by the formalities.

Margaret kept roughly wiping her tears away. It made it so hard to see. Somehow she believed she should be able to ride right up to Rachel and take her home. She had gotten her fill of this trip. These countless old mining roads riddling the area made a thorough search by two riders impossible.

She urged Kestrel up yet another trail. The mare must be getting tired, she thought; she was more and more reluctant to respond to Margaret's urging.

Kate pushed Chalk up to ride next to Kestrel. "You know," she said thoughtfully, "I can't see her just riding off the main trail. She's too experienced a competitor to miss the markers... unless they weren't there."

Margaret and Kate stared at each other. "Let's ride back toward your pit stop and see if anyone has taken down the markers," Margaret said, feeling strength flow into herself.

Without another word they rode the rest of the way to Devil's Thumb, following the ribbons in reverse. *All hanging.* Margaret had to fight to keep herself from sinking again.

Nearing the pit stop Kate checked her watch. "It's close to six. Maybe there's a note for us."

Kestrel absolutely refused to go the twenty feet or so off the trail to their pit stop. Margaret told Kate, "You go. I'll wait here." Stroking the mare's neck she murmured, "Poor Kestrel. I know you're tired, but you must keep going until we find her."

Kate came running back moments later, excitedly waving the note. She called out, "They've been here, they think the same thing, that somebody's taken the trail markers down. It says here to take the trail that branches off to the right, about a hundred yards from here. June says they are sure Rachel went that way."

"Let's go, then." Margaret said. "We only have about three hours of daylight left."

When they reached the place it was obvious—there wasn't a yellow ribbon in sight. Kestrel eagerly took the trail. When it leveled off she balked. Margaret thought, I shouldn't have ridden her up the steep hill. Kate studied the mare curiously. Kestrel turned to the left and took a few steps. Margaret pulled the right rein and gave her a little kick. A surprised *oof* came from the horse. Margaret tried again to get her back onto the trail.

Kestrel clamped her teeth on the bit, lowered her head, and stood fast. Kate was trying to fit this side of Kestrel into what she knew of her. It didn't work. In Kate's experience, this mare had never refused to move forward. She didn't look tired, just stubborn.

Margaret jumped off and tied the reins to a tree branch. "We'll just have to leave her here. She's much too exhausted to go on." She turned and walked a short way up the trail while Kate stayed, watching the mare. Kestrel was now dancing around in half circles, pawing the ground vigorously. She raised her head and snorted her frustration, then gave a ringing neigh.

"We've been making a big mistake, Margaret," Kate said excitedly, "I think she's been trying to take us to Rachel all along. Get back on and give her her head."

Margaret's face changed from annoyance at this interruption in her search to an awareness that she had been deaf to the mare. Untying the reins, she scrambled into the saddle, then made it clear to Kestrel that she was finally in charge.

Leaving the trail at a trot, Kestrel angled downhill. When she came to the downed timber she put her head to the ground and cast back and forth like a retriever. She turned in a spin that almost unhorsed Margaret to go back uphill at a different angle, her nose still to the ground.

"This is where it happened," Kate said, anxiety and possibility mixed in her voice. "Let's spread out from each other a bit."

Riding up ahead and to the right, Kate vaulted off the mule when she spotted the bright red fanny pack wedged between an exposed root and a rock. She shouted "Hey!" as she snatched it up and saw a broken piece of leather rein dangling from the pack's smashed buckle.

She turned to find Margaret standing next to Kestrel, holding something in her hand. Kate ran over to her, practically dragging Chalk behind her. It was a piece of brown rag. "Oh, no." Her stomach seized and sank like a lead weight. It was Rachel's gayly boastful Big Sky T-shirt, or rather a blood-soaked shred of it. Kate looked at Margaret's face. It was drained of blood, as if it had left her face and flowed out through her hand into this scrap of cloth.

Almost simultaneously it came home to both of them that Rachel was probably dead. They were suddenly filled with the dread of finding her. Neither one wanted to be alone when it happened.

Margaret tilted her head back and yelled, "Rachel!" Only the *chel-chel-chel* echoed back from the canyons. She sank down to the ground, the tiny wildflowers strange company for the rag in her hand.

Kate's clear voice cut through to Margaret. "We only have a couple more hours of daylight left. Wait here. I'm going to try to raise June and Mollie with the police whistle." She spoke gently. "It will only take me a few minutes. I want to leave a marker of some kind out at the trail. When I get back we'll start looking. O.K?" Getting a small nod, she left.

Kate returned quickly. She found Margaret still in the same place staring at the rag. Kate softly pried open her fingers, took the thing, and threw it behind her. In a firm voice she said, "It's time to start looking for Rachel."

When the sky was pink, but the canyon they were working their way into was dark shadowy blues, they were joined by June and Mollie. The fresh help was needed to decipher the faint traces of Rachel's passage. Flashlights were necessary now. Every place that could conceal a body was checked.

They fanned out and worked a little faster. It was full dark by the time they reached the water. Mollie found it first by slipping down the bank, landing surprised knee deep in the frigid stuff. "Whoops. This water's one degree hotter than ice cubes." They could hear splashes accented by the wild sweep of her flashlight as she tried to find a place to climb out. Then a loud clear, "Well, I'll be damned. Hey, girls, I've found her brassiere." She held it high for all their flashlights to converge their beams on, like searchlights on a bomber during the London blitz.

There was a general flood of relief that they had not missed Rachel and that she was mobile enough to have gotten this far— far enough to drink. Urgency surged through the group.

"All right," Margaret said, "we know she must be in the river or on the banks. Let's spread out. Check each bank. And pool. And move as fast as we can."

When Rachel opened her eyes she felt a moment of panic. She couldn't see. Then she remembered pulling herself onto a sandbar in the last half-light of the deep canyon's day. The dark night had moved around her like a tight fist. The water kept her company with a mindless chattering around the small stones by her head, and a rich baritone rumble from the larger rocks out in the current. But she had finally had enough of water.

A wracking shiver of cold made her teeth clack. Making an effort to sit up, she whimpered with the pain, to sink back to the gravel with sobs of pure helplessness.

A drumming sound from overhead stopped her crying. A helicopter. There must be search parties out, she thought. She wouldn't die here. Someone would find her. The drumming stopped, then came again. Her ears tried to sort the sounds out of the dark. The suspension bridge! She was directly under it.

"Help!" she cried, but knew it hardly carried over the sounds of the water flowing past her head. Waiting until the next time she heard a horse on the bridge she filled her lungs to yell again. Lying spent from the extreme effort, she could hear the faint sounds of hoofbeats fading away. No one could hear her puny call from way down here, she decided. The cold made it very difficult for her to control her jaw to yell, and the shivering was exhausting her. She lay back to rest her cheek and breasts against the cold round stones.

The line of flashlights moved raggedly down the canyon, Margaret and Mollie taking wading duty, Kate on one bank, June on the other.

It was as if the flashlights found her of their own accord, sniffing along like the mare. They caressed her once with their yellow beams, then found and held her, lit on the island of gravel.

For a flash of a second no one wanted to be the first to touch her, to feel the rubbery skin and search out the nonexistent pulse. Then Margaret made some primitive sound. She struggled against the water. Her feet seemed weighted down, the uneven, slippery stones making her awkward, ungainly.

She fell forward onto her knees when she reached the sandbar, unaware of how that hurt, reaching deep inside herself for the courage to know.

Her fingers searched for and found the proof of Rachel's heart beating. It wasn't strong, but it was there. She felt more than saw the tent the other three women formed over them. Margaret looked up, her eyes hollow from lack of sleep and fear.

"We have to get her out of here. She's suffering from hypothermia along with. . ." Margaret's flashlight illuminated Rachel's gruesome back, "these wounds." Her voice threatened to get shrill. "How are we going to get her out of here?" she said, sweeping her light up the sheer walls.

Mollie said, "We'll use the mules," and started to go get them. Kate held out a hand to stop her. "No," she said, "I'll go. I'll be faster. Which ones?"

"Bring Chalk and Sherpa. No, wait. Bring them all, Kestrel too. The best thing is to go out to June's airplane. We can pick up the Peavine Road by following this river upstream a short ways. Yeah, that's best."

Kate's young adrenalin-pushed legs were already splashing up through the water when Mollie yelled after her, "Tie Sherpa to Chalk's tail."

Trying to be very gentle and careful, the three women managed to move Rachel to a fairly level place. June, with great tenderness, wrapped Rachel's upper body with her own windbreaker.

Rachel stirred and said, "Mother?"

All of their clothes were wet. The cold wind made their teeth chatter, like a far-from-festive mariachi band. Mollie swiftly dug a depression in the sandy soil, then gathered leaves and pine needles to fill it. They placed Rachel there. Margaret found a plastic garbage bag caught in bushes by the river. She split it open to cover Rachel. The three women huddled together for warmth while they waited.

When Kate returned, Kestrel pushed her way to Rachel, lowered her nose, and with fluttering nostrils examined her person. She gave a soft whicker, a mare to foal call, then raised her head to look at Kate. "Yes," Kate answered.

It took them three more hours to pack her out, lashed between Chalk and Sherpa, cocooned in a makeshift horse-blanket stretcher. Mollie led them over Cockoo Ridge, down the Peavine Road, ending up at the Cedars airport. Carefully, Rachel was transferred to the cargo space of June's plane. Kate offered to help Mollie with the mules and Kestrel, hauling them out to the stables at Auburn. Mollie allowed she could use the help.

The thrumming roar of the small plane brought the others back to civilization. Even June seemed overwhelmed by all the dials on the instrument panel, in their usual places before her. Margaret climbed into the plane out of the cold night air, her hands having difficulty with the simple tasks asked of them. She slid down under the blanket next to Rachel to try to warm her. Wanting to hold her but afraid of hurting her, she watched Rachel's face faintly lit from the instrument panel lights.

The drone of the plane was seducing the part of Margaret's brain that was demanding sleep. Her brain felt like a large mucousy oyster wanting to slip out of the confines of her skull.

Her head jerked, and she opened her eyes to find Rachel's eyes open and dark, looking directly at her. Margaret had the sense that she was not really aware of her surroundings. Leaning near to be heard over the plane's engine, she said, "You're going to be all right. June is flying you to the hospital. This is your sweetie talking. I love you, darling. Stay here with us." She kept talking as long as Rachel's eyes were open, then sang lullabies until the plane landed at Auburn.

Twenty-One

"**N**o, I'm sorry. No visitors are allowed while the patient is in Intensive Care. Except, of course, for immediate family, or spouse. Is Mrs. Duncan's husband here?" The nurse aimed her eyes over the hairline of her bifocals at Margaret.

"It is Ms. Duncan." Margaret briefly entertained saying, *I'm her spouse,* or something similar. She had to admit, however, that she did not have the energy to see it through. She also worried that the resulting epidemic of homophobia would affect Rachel's care.

Standing behind the fortlike nurse's station in her beloved overalls, Margaret knew they had lost some of their appeal over the last forty-eight hours. After trustingly turning Rachel over to the emergency room staff, Margaret had spent the remainder of the night on a plastic couch placed between two palms, the musak punctuated by a nasal-voiced pager. By dawn she was deeply into fantasies involving surgical removal of the pager's vocal cords. But she had not realized until this moment that Rachel had entered some prison, with doctors as wardens and nurses as guards.

"Well," she took a deep, calm breath, "tell me how she is."

"I'm sorry, we can't give out that kind of information except—"

Margaret blew. "I know you must feel that regulations come from a higher power but"—easy now, she thought—"don't you understand that Rachel is here with her friends? She has no living relatives, she's not from this area. We are concerned about her, and it may be reassuring to her that we're here." Margaret closed with her best bureaucrat-pleasing smile.

The nurse picked up a paper, scanning it in an ostentatiously preoccupied way. Then she put it with others and smacked them on the countertop, aligning the edges. "Sorry, my dear, but I can't change the rules."

Margaret breathed in lungfuls of air, changing her shape before the nurse's eyes from a sagging wilderness traveler into a tall, powerful Amazonian warrior. "Who can?"

Turning the frail stem on her tidy gold watch, the nurse, of a mettle to withstand the onslaught of wild horses, said, "Dr. Briggs will be in at nine o'clock. She will be taking charge of the patient."

She scanned Margaret, starting with her disheveled hair, bypassing the eyes, leaning slightly against the counter to see below the waist. She shook her head slightly.

Lifting her chin one-half inch, Margaret said, "Tell her to page Dr. Carson when she arrives." In an instant she could see that she had found the password.

"Yes, Doctor, I will, just as soon as she comes in."

Margaret walked to the center of the waiting room to stand, motionless eyes fixed on the wall mural of the area's goldmining history. Barely recognizable donkeys and miners conveniently hidden behind sagebrush were suspended in an improbable landscape. *A struggling local artist, no doubt.*

She nodded her head in a slow thoughtful way as though appreciating the value of the painting, or its message. If throwing my DVM around will get me in to see Rachel, she thought, then maybe I need to look the part. Margaret glanced at her watch. Eight-ten. She had time to go to her as-yet-pristine motel room, take a shower, and dress in clothes in her duffel bag that would enhance her image. *Power suit* was the new term. Well, she would use it, this foxy style, to get into the hen house.

At the motel Margaret learned that June was still sleeping. Kate and Mollie had not yet checked in. She left a message for them, picked up her key, entered her impersonal room to find that June had unpacked her bags for her and hung the clothes she had brought for the awards banquet in the closet. How considerate, Margaret thought.

Catching her unexpected reflection in the big mirror over the dresser, she briefly wondered who that haggard woman was. Leaning closer she could see the purplish blush under the lower eyelid, the grime-filled wrinkles, the tangled hair. Blood from a scratch on her neck had darkened her collar. She laughed. "No wonder that nurse wouldn't let me past the front barrier. She's probably worried I'd contaminate the whole hospital," she said to the honest glass.

Striding back through the silently sliding electric doors at 9:01 walked a dragonfly woman. An iridescent illusion had been created in the motel room. Margaret's suit, a natural raw silk, flowed on her body in tailored elegance. Showing briefly with each stride, her dark mahogany boots rang with authority across the tiles. Under the lapel-less jacket she wore a white silk blouse. A scarf came in handy to cover the scratch. It was the dragonfly wing—blues and greens with a streak of red-gold like her hair.

The whoosh of electric doors moved behind her, more an exchange of air than a sound. She turned to see a small, fine-boned, pale woman in her mid-thirties, with shoulder-length brown hair that was stringy from going at least two days longer than its desired wash day. The nurse's voice came from the ramparts, "Good morning, Dr. Briggs. Dr. Carson here wishes to see you about a patient admitted last night. A Miss Duncan."

Margaret tried manufacturing a smile as she held her hand out to shake Dr. Briggs'. What entered the warmth of her fingers was limp and cold, reptilelike.

"How do you do. Ms. Duncan, my friend, and I are here from Montana. She was riding in the Tevis Cup," explained Margaret. "She became lost and was injured, suffering from dehydration and hypothermia—"

"Yes, yes." She was interrupted by Dr. Briggs who obviously did not like being told her business. While Margaret had been talking Dr. Briggs picked up a clipboard with an attached chart. Now, in the silence, she read the night physician's notes.

"I would like to see her and be kept informed of her condition," Margaret finished boldly. Out of the corner of her eye she could see the nurse marshalling herself for one last try.

"Dr. Briggs, she's not a relative of the patient."

Dr. Briggs looked up from her charts, seeing only the uniform. "That's all right Miss. . .um. She's a doctor." Turning to Margaret, she said, "You could come along with me now while I examine her."

Margaret couldn't look at the nurse. She felt no triumph at her treatment. This woman would never have a name even if she wore a nametag every day.

"What's your specialty?" she heard Dr. Briggs ask.

"General. However, lately I've considered going into sports medicine." Their shoes rang off the floor as they walked down the hall, sometimes in unison, sometimes in ragged separation. Margaret dreaded the next question usually asked, *Where did you train?* She knew she couldn't say Cornell. Deep inside, Margaret was fighting to keep control of her worry for Rachel and her longing to hold her and be comforted by her presence. She hated this game, but it had gotten her past the alligators. The drawbridge was down.

As they neared the end of the hall Margaret could sense the increasing presence of the Intensive Care Unit. Lights that were always on, a twenty-four-hour place with no regard for seasons, moons, eclipses. A different rhythmic beat hung in the air, of hearts and brain waves. And the machines that monitored them.

They stopped at the ICU command island. Margaret tensely scanned her surroundings. Dr. Briggs conferred with the head nurse.

Everything fell away for Margaret—Dr. Briggs, the sterile surroundings, her rampart-breaching game—when she saw, through a large monitoring window, a shape on a bed that she knew was Rachel. It was as if her eyes drew all of her through the glass to the sheet-muffled form.

Rachel seemed flattened in the high bed. She was lying on her stomach, her head turned away. A nurse moved around in the room.

Margaret tried to tune her ears to the conversation going on beside her, but they were talking about a broken leg. Feeling impatient, she made a slight move toward the open door to Rachel.

"Dr. Carson," Margaret heard the thin voice of Dr. Briggs, "I must check on an interesting multiple fracture case that arrived this morning before I see your friend. She is quite out of danger, you know." Relief surrounded Margaret like a bubble-filled bath. "Would you like to come with me while I examine the trauma patient?"

The consternation on Margaret's face told Dr. Briggs more than the slight negative shake of her head.

"Fine," the doctor continued, "go on in to see her. I'll be along shortly."

Margaret rounded the doorjamb, skirted the end of the bed, and saw Rachel's face. In this hard light she was barely recognizable; the moon had been kinder. Her eyes opened and flooded with relief at the sight of Margaret. They held each other through their eyes. This was what they had both needed—to reassure each other they were in the world.

Rachel struggled to free her hand from the tightly tucked-in sheet. It was like a cat who had crawled under the covers only to find that it suddenly wanted out. Margaret helped her work it loose and found that its goal was her own hand. She lowered her cheek to the coarse white weave of the hospital blanket and cried.

Rachel looked at the top of her lover's head. She felt her nearness so strongly that she realized, with a powerful certainty, she always wanted Margaret in her life. In fact, she needed her. Rachel had fought away this need, had believed that if she relied on anyone else it made her weak, vulnerable. She did not have to do it all alone anymore, to be so damned perfect. She was ruthless in her standards of perfection for herself, and her critical awareness of flaws in the people around her had kept her separated from them.

Rachel remembered the lemonade incident with her father that had surfaced on the hot slope, the feelings of shame at her father's words. He had not been able to accept weakness in her, however temporary. She thought, I've been living that out for myself all these years. I didn't need him around to do it. I learned his language well and have kept his voice inside me.

Margaret raised her head and smiled. Her tears had washed the make-up away in streaks. Rachel could see the tangible signs of exhaustion.

"Go to bed," Rachel croaked out, "darling." She lay palely on the white sheet, white hospital gown tied at the back of her neck.

Margaret nodded, then leaned close to whisper, "The bride wore white."

The wrinkles on the outside corners of Rachel's eyes deepened. The lips made a few twitches.

"Ahemmm," a white thunder cloud rumbled. "It's time for our rest."

"I'll say," Margaret said to the nurse as she stood. She leaned over to kiss Rachel on her cheek, avoiding the white ointment-smeared lips. She had turned to follow the nurse's squeaky shoes across the floor when she heard a small voice and turned back.

"Take me home," made it weakly across the distance.

Margaret stared at her hard, then nodded.

In the wake of Margaret's visit Rachel lay curled on the soft sheets, feeling warm, dry, and loved. She picked up the key to herself she had found laying on the slope and carefully turned back to the memories of her father.

There she found an ordinary man. As his daughter she had needed him to be more than ordinary: a western cowboy-hero parent, perfect in every respect. It seemed the more terrible his behavior became the more fiercely she would defend him, the more perfect he had to be. Until her loyalty made his image into a stranger. Then everything collapsed.

Seeing him as a flawed adult, not as a parent, changed her relationship to him from that of child to another adult. Rachel felt lightheaded with relief. It was as if an old, overgrown concept had moved out. Now she found much more room for herself.

Twenty-Two

Mollie hung back like a mule on the end of its lead rope as June led the way to the main desk. Rachel had been out of intensive care since around noon and had been moved to a room. June asked directions.

As she waited, Mollie's eyes shifted down each of the three long halls leading off from the nurse's desk. She sought out horizons, hawks, and coming storms, but saw only the long polished bareness of the linoleum with occasional loaded carts parked against the walls. Taking a step back toward the glass barrier that slid silently, holding her world at bay, she felt a strong urge to leave June to the visiting. Her mind started forming some reason she would have to wait out near Tin Lezzie.

June knew her well. With a certain tough gentleness she took Mollie's elbow. "Come on, you old reprobate. I'll make sure they don't confuse you with a patient about to croak. I guarantee I'll get you back out of here." Mollie wavered a bit, then stomped down the corridor with a fierce and darting look.

The doors measured their stride, small black numbers centered on each one, until they found the room holding Rachel. The relief they felt as they ducked in through the open door was mixed when they actually saw Rachel. It is unnerving to see a friend one day—vital, exuberant, in the pink—and the next day have her be pale, bandaged, wounded, with only enough spare energy to lift one hand from the wrist and squeak out, "Hi."

They talked about the things Rachel hungered to hear, the things that made her life a reality. Rachel asked about Kestrel, and about the results of the race. June said she had stopped in at the awards ceremony that afternoon where she had heard some juicy news for Rachel.

"Seems that Dwight back-talked the judge at Michigan Bluff when she pulled his horse from the race. She told him she had never seen such severe bit injuries. That his gelding was the most dehydrated to pass through that day. He raged around trashing the judging teams, the ride, everything, but she set him down sharp and fast. Told him she would see to it that next year his entry would not be considered. He had some cooling out to do while waiting for his transport out."

"There's a man that talks before he thinks," Mollie said.

"I'll say. And do you know, Kate told me that sorry excuse for a human being made some claim that it was Rachel's fault his horse was in that shape?"

"Guess I was . . . poor beast. Must have drug me a ways from the bit in his mouth," Rachel said.

June nodded, thoughtfully. "I think you got the worst end of the bargain."

"Going to give it a try again next year?" Mollie asked.

"Since you were bumped I'd guess you would automatically be on next year's starters list," June said to Rachel.

"Not if she broke their goddamn rules." Mollie looked around for a place to spit.

"I think," said June, "if she had finished it might have been a different story, especially if she had bested the best. Now they can just pretend she wasn't there." She looked softly and fondly at her friend, then patted the shoulder not mounded by gauze bandages. "Next year."

Rachel nodded, the need gone from her eyes but the desire still there. "Did anything about Kestrel and me get in the newspaper?" she asked.

"I looked at the paper over breakfast. Nothing about you in it. Your friend Janet Reardon must have decided it was a nonstarter."

Rachel raised her eyebrows. "What about you two?"

"I'm going to stay with Mollie a few days, but then we are going to look more closely at where our future together is headed." She felt Mollie's arm move across the back of her chair to give

June a small squeeze. June was in shock. Mollie had never been demonstrative in public before.

Mollie nodded, her brown eyes thoughtful and serious. "I liked hang'n out with you guys. Feels like a gang, ya know?" She laughed her big laugh, the sound bouncing off the white enclosure startling them all. Her eyes slid nervously to the door. "Wouldn't mind do'n more of it. It don't have to be so dramatic, though." She smiled cautiously, wary another laugh might escape to shatter the sober hospital background noise. "I could do packing in Montana as well as California."

Kate came in as the supper trolleys were making their rounds, the evening light slanting in through the closed window. The drone of the air conditioner took the sharp edges off sound and filtered out all earth smells. The two old gals stood by the bed, Mollie turning her Stetson constantly.

Mollie said, "Let's git." Nodding at Kate as she edged toward the door, she squeezed by the trolley almost blocking her escape. "See ya later, gals. It's been fun."

June, eyeing her lover's retreat, knew she would find her in the parking lot. "I'll come visit you in a month, and I want to see you on the back of a horse by that time, you hear? While I'm there I'll take a look at that mare you think will retire Madge." She gave a snort of disbelief. " 'Course, I'd have to hire a horse shrink to help Madge through her feelings of sibling rivalry and abandonment. Heh, heh. Well, see you around. Bye, Kate."

Kate sat in a chair by the bed. Rachel smiled a pleased welcome, then turned her head to see if Margaret had come in with her. Kate laughed. "She is still sleeping off over fifty hours of excitement. She crashed into bed this morning muttering something about you being in prison and we had to spring you."

"Still in intensive care this morning." Rachel formed the words carefully. Her lips, swollen and cracked, were so greasy with ointment she never knew exactly where they would meet. Kate had to lean near to understand her. "How you feeling?"

"Pretty slow."

Wanting to help Rachel somehow, Kate lifted the lid from a plate on the tray. "Jeez, what's this? I thought it would be food."

"Lunch wasn't any better," Rachel responded. "I'll eat the

jello."

"I guess you might want some help with this?" Kate looked the question at Rachel, who gave her back a grateful nod. Kate put a couple of pillows under Rachel's chest, then tried with uneven success to spoon jello into her mouth. After scraping a few of the shimmering red squares off the sheets into the wastepaper basket, Kate commented, "Slippery little devils, aren't they?" When the bowl was emptied Kate said, "Kestrel will wonder how long you'll be laid up."

Rachel shook her head. She shrugged her shoulders, then winced. "Don't know," she groaned.

"Don't worry," Kate reassured her employer. "I'll take care of you. And the rest of the stock."

It was a tremendous coup Margaret pulled off. She could have papered her apartment walls with the disclaimers she signed Monday afternoon. She had ten hours of sleep behind her, and Rachel had progressed to hobbling up and down the halls. After Kate had been in to see her over dinnertime she had said to Margaret, "We have to get her out of there before the food finishes her off."

Tuesday morning the truck and horse trailer pulled up to the main entrance of the hospital. Margaret pushed Rachel in her wheelchair through the glass doors, whooshing like the opening curtain at the Metropolitan Opera. Almost the full staff of the Auburn Community Hospital watched as Kate dropped the ramp. Margaret wheeled Rachel into the horse trailer. Rachel rose, patted her mare's rump, then slid down to crawl into her sleeping bag and straw bed made up in the stall beside Kestrel with a look of absolute contentment. The familiar sounds and smells surrounded her. Kestrel kept up a constant rumbling greeting as the hospital staff fretted in a half circle around the trailer's rear, like a flock of white ducks.

Dr. Briggs kept shaking her head, very unsatisfied with the sanitation. She pointed to traces of manure on the open ramp, "This just won't do. Transporting my patient in an open cesspool. When that horse has to urinate—" At the *u* word a hush fell on the murmuring hospital staff. One of the orderlies voiced his concern about the possibility Rachel would be stepped upon by the horse.

Margaret closed the ramp and firmly bolted it as she tried to field questions. "No, the horse won't trample her to death. I don't think you will need to worry about the urine. We put a sheet of plastic under the straw."

She marched around to the truck cab to let Kate know they were ready. They exchanged grins of total triumph. Margaret entered the small door on the front of the trailer to settle in her nest at Rachel's head. Kate smoothly left the hospital behind and took the ramp up to 80 East. They were headed for home.

Kestrel's tail flowed over the top of the tailgate like a jet stream.

Other titles from Firebrand Books include:

Artemis In Echo Park, Poetry by Eloise Klein Healy/$8.95
Before Our Eyes, A Novel by Joan Alden/$8.95
Beneath My Heart, Poetry by Janice Gould/$8.95
The Big Mama Stories by Shay Youngblood/$8.95
The Black Back-Ups, Poetry by Kate Rushin/$8.95
A Burst Of Light, Essays by Audre Lorde/$8.95
Cecile, Stories by Ruthann Robson/$8.95
Crime Against Nature, Poetry by Minnie Bruce Pratt/$8.95
Diamonds Are A Dyke's Best Friend by Yvonne Zipter/$9.95
Dykes To Watch Out For, Cartoons by Alison Bechdel/$7.95
Dykes To Watch Out For: The Sequel, Cartoons by Alison Bechdel/$9.95
Exile In The Promised Land, A Memoir by Marcia Freedman/$8.95
Experimental Love, Poetry by Cheryl Clarke/$8.95
Eye Of A Hurricane, Stories by Ruthann Robson/$8.95
The Fires Of Bride, A Novel by Ellen Galford/$8.95
Food & Spirits, Stories by Beth Brant (Degonwadonti)/$8.95
Forty-Three Septembers, Essays by Jewelle Gomez/$10.95
Free Ride, A Novel by Marilyn Gayle/$9.95
A Gathering Of Spirit, A Collection by North American Indian Women
   edited by Beth Brant (Degonwadonti)/$10.95
Getting Home Alive by Aurora Levins Morales and Rosario Morales/$9.95
The Gilda Stories, A Novel by Jewelle Gomez/$9.95
Good Enough To Eat, A Novel by Lesléa Newman/$8.95
Humid Pitch, Narrative Poetry by Cheryl Clarke/$8.95
Jewish Women's Call For Peace edited by Rita Falbel, Irena Klepfisz, and
   Donna Nevel/$4.95
Jonestown & Other Madness, Poetry by Pat Parker/$7.95
Just Say Yes, A Novel by Judith McDaniel/$9.95
The Land Of Look Behind, Prose and Poetry by Michelle Cliff/$8.95
Legal Tender, A Mystery by Marion Foster/$9.95
Lesbian (Out)law, Survival Under the Rule of Law by Ruthann Robson/$9.95
A Letter To Harvey Milk, Short Stories by Lesléa Newman/$9.95
Letting In The Night, A Novel by Joan Lindau/$8.95
Living As A Lesbian, Poetry by Cheryl Clarke/$7.95
Metamorphosis, Reflections on Recovery by Judith McDaniel/$7.95
Mohawk Trail by Beth Brant (Degonwadonti)/$7.95
Moll Cutpurse, A Novel by Ellen Galford/$7.95
The Monarchs Are Flying, A Novel by Marion Foster/$8.95
More Dykes To Watch Out For, Cartoons by Alison Bechdel/$7.95
Movement In Black, Poetry by Pat Parker/$8.95
My Mama's Dead Squirrel, Lesbian Essays on Southern Culture by Mab
   Segrest/ $9.95
New, Improved! Dykes To Watch Out For, Cartoons by Alison Bechdel/$8.95
Normal Sex by Linda Smukler/$8.95